# Make Me A Hero

## Also by Jerome Brooks

The Big Dipper Marathon
The Testing of Charlie Hammelman
Uncle Mike's Boy

# ★ Make Me ★ A Hero

★

by JEROME BROOKS

AN AUTHORS GUILD BACKINPRINT.COM EDITION

*Make Me A Hero*

All Rights Reserved © 1980, 2000 by Jerome Brooks

AN AUTHORS GUILD BACKINPRINT.COM EDITION

Published by iUniverse.com, Inc.

For information address:
iUniverse.com, Inc.
620 North 48th Street, Suite 201
Lincoln, NE 68504-3467
www.iuniverse.com

Originally published by E. P. Dutton

Edited by Ann Durell
Designed by Claire Counihan

ISBN: 0-595-09434-1

Printed in the United States of America

**for my parents**

# Chapter 1

Maybe it was the accident with Chris that started the whole thing.

Who knows?

Jake, it's true, was only seven then. The war hadn't even started and the two Bar Mitzvahs were still such distant things they weren't yet things at all.

As for the shop and Harry Katz—well, they were less far off than the Bar Mitzvahs. But even so, they played a part in all of it. And on that Saturday afternoon, returning from the five-and-ten with his mother, clutching the lead soldier in his hand and dreaming of all the brave things a soldier could be that he, Jacob Ackerman, couldn't, how was he supposed to know that within seconds, the two of them—his mother and he—would come upon the accident and that it would tie the war and the shop and Harry and the Bar Mitzvahs all so tightly together they would never be able to be separated again?

Who knows about such things in advance?

They just happen—separately, discretely, in isolation from each other—then end up, four, five, six years later, all bunched up in a single moment of fear and shame, anger and, at the last, knowledge.

Like the day with Chris and the telephone pole.

The sky was so blue when that happened, it hurt the eyes just to look up at it through the elm trees. Birds chirped madly, really enjoying the first days of spring, their first leaps into freedom from the prison of the nest, scudding through the air like dark little clouds blown by the wind. The air was warm with the smell of bursting forsythia and tulips, and the streets were filled with pastel people aglow with relief over the death of winter.

Jake's mother was just saying, as they turned the corner from Division Street to Francisco Avenue, in the broken English he had to admit embarrassed him, *"Tsk, tsk!* Soldiers! I don't understand it. A boat I can understand. A balloon I can understand. But to walk five blocks to buy a toy soldier? Who holds a gun in the hand, yet, too? Who can understand it?"

She was little and fat and her hair pitch-black and cut short at the neck so that, from the back, the neck leading to the hair looked like a bewhiskered chin. When she spoke there was the usual shrillness in her voice, as though she were at the threshold of some crisis.

Jake recoiled from the shrillness by clutching the lead soldier even more tightly, feeling the sharpness of the burrs along the soldier's arms and legs, and planning how, with the four other soldiers he'd already collected, he could stage a fantastic battle on the porcelain-covered kitchen table, using the new soldier, with the fierce-looking eyes and the impressive epaulets, as the leader to take the others on a charge over a hill molded of clay. He could scarcely wait to rush up the flight of stairs to the apartment—praying the kitchen would be empty.

But the instant they turned the corner and were walled in by the rows of two- and three-story flats on either side of Francisco, he sensed that the battle on the kitchen table would have to be delayed. For there, towards the middle of the sun-stroked, speckled vista, was a stirring—of the sort associated with fire engines or police cars or ambulances. A crowd, a circle of craned necks, tense with anticipation, fraught with fear or admiration or both, surrounded the telephone pole that stood just to the right of the haunted house, the house that wasn't really a house at all, only the foundation of one, but was house enough for them all to use as a fort during the day and as a ghoulish castle at night or on Halloween. The stirring rippled outward, setting Jake's arms atingle with premonitions and sorrowful omens.

Someone's going up the pole, he thought. And then, wistfully, Darn! I wish I had guts like that.

His mother simply shook her pitch-black, close-cropped head and *tsk*ed several more times. This was not her kind of crisis. Telephone-pole climbers had nothing to do with Cossacks rampaging through little Polish villages in the dark of night, looking for young girls to sate themselves on. How she loved to retell those stories of her childhood early in the century! How Jake loved to listen!

Her pace neither slackened nor quickened. Her destination and objective remained the same: the apartment and preparation for the Saturday-evening meal, as elaborate a ritual for her as the Friday housecleaning in anticipation of the Sabbath. She shrugged her shoulders as they neared the circle of bodies, not even deigning to acknowledge with a sidelong glance at the pole that something unusual—maybe a seed that in several years would explode—was awakening Francisco Avenue from its more typical lethargy.

Jake, though, stopped—abruptly. "I'm staying," he said,

3

caught up already in the muted, reverent, awed and fascinated excitement of the crowd.

The hand with which she'd been clasping his slipped away with quivering reluctance, as much as to say, "I know! I know! You're the last. You're the youngest. Like the other three, it's time now for you, too, to go. So how—why—should I stop you? I couldn't hold them back either."

For a moment—shamed, guilt-struck—Jake hesitated, his arm hovering in midair. He stood transfixed, torn by an instinct to reclutch the empty hand dangling by his mother's side. But the pull of the tiny figure inching its way up the pole was greater than the pull of duty or love or both. Almost apologetically, he said, "It's Chris. Chris Petropolous, Mama." As though, hearing the name, she would magically come to see that some things were more important than others.

She smiled, but not so clearly that he could be sure she understood, and, with her empty hand still dangling limply by her side, left him behind to merge into the crowd.

Howie Woscowicz, from the first-floor apartment, was the one he ended up leaning against—not by plan or intention, but accidentally, as though some higher power had fated it, had seen it as the best way to really make the thing hurt more, sink deeper into him so that it would become, six years later at the time of the Bar Mitzvah, an unforgettable, tormenting memory.

"Sucker!" Howie growled, eyeing the figure of Chris Petropolous as it grew more and more diminutive against the dazzling sky and the parallel lines of the telephone wires. "Goddamn sucker, taking me up on a dare like that, trying to show everyone he's not a puny little bastard after all! Well, let him get down. We'll beat the shit out of him anyway."

Jake's fingers gripped the epauleted soldier more tightly,

but it wasn't enough. He couldn't squeeze it enough to still the fear he shuddered with—fear for what awaited Chris at Howie's hands when he got down, because Howie was not in the habit of making idle threats. The business in the park, with Jake caged under the upside-down mesh litter basket, hadn't been an idle threat.

Howie had said to the others—Gene and Stash—"Let's piss on him." And Jake had gripped the tiny triangles of wire with all his might, thinking, It's just a joke. They want to scare me is all. If I hold on tight enough, they'll go away.

But they hadn't. And when he looked up inside the cage, at the wooden bottom with the tiny drain hole, he wanted to laugh. The hole looked so small, how could anyone put the thing through it and urinate? Only, with Gene and Stash holding the cage down tightly and sneering through the wire mesh, Howie had pulled it out and fit it through the hole, and Jake, startled by the truth of what was happening, looked up at it just in time to feel the smelly, humiliating water streaming into his eyes.

So now he kept his eyes on tiny Chris and prayed, either that he got to the top and stayed until they all forgot about him or else came down victorious, shouting to them all— Howie and Gene and Stash—that tough guys couldn't go around interfering with a person's pride and integrity.

Only Chris kept climbing. Hand over hand. Leg circled above leg. Clinging to the splintery pole past the point where it might have been possible, with grace even and a certain pride in having gone as high as he had already, to come back down and pretend it hadn't happened.

Breaths all around came a little more rapidly. Jake's was accompanied by a cold sweat that forced him as subtly as he could, so Howie wouldn't notice, to raise his free hand to his forehead in a desperate effort to erase any signs of concern.

5

But he needn't have bothered. Even Howie was into the whole thing so much now, the sweat had broken out on his forehead too. "Damned sucker!" he moaned. "Dumb squirt's going to kill himself yet. We won't have to do anything."

The silence grew staggering. Chris had passed the last of the iron rungs sticking out from the pole, and now only sheer willpower and strength drove him upward.

A woman shrieked from a window across the street. "Why doesn't somebody get him down for godsakes! Why are you all gawking? Get him down before he kills himself!"

The words hung in the air over all of them like a heavy, oppressive shroud that they were just too paralyzed to lift.

Even Jake, whose head was like an echo chamber where *kills,* inexorably and absolutely trapped, ricocheted back and forth, stood frozen next to the landlord's son, whom he guessed he hated as much as anything in the world.

He found himself muttering, "Come on, Chris. You can make it."

Chris's hand stretched, groped for the uppermost part of the pole. His dark, petrified face turned frantically for an instant to glance down at the assembly. His eyes were filled with disbelief, as though this thing couldn't actually be happening at all, as though it were some kind of mistake that had suddenly been recognized for what it was.

But a sparrow, seeking a place to alight, skittered past his shoulder. A gray, drowsy, unthinking sparrow, swooping down, then up past his shoulder. Chris twitched, as if to frighten it away from this domain that was his to conquer—this bird that, by its antics, was interfering with pride and integrity and that final resolve by which one demonstrates to the whole world of Francisco Avenue that even shrimps and

**6**

squirts and kids who clench lead soldiers in their hands have certain inalienable rights.

All it took was a second or one-thousandth of a second. The hand—outreached, outstretched—to scare the bird or to find a secure thing to clutch, missed. And the encircling legs, squeezing the weathered pole for life, loosened, slacked off a bit. And the wail—that would last through the war, through the shop, through the first meeting with Harry Katz and the Bar Mitzvahs—began.

Oh, what an excruciating wail. "O-o-o-o-o-h!" Drawn out long and peaky all the way from the top of that pole down its splintery length, past the iron rungs, to the sidewalk below. Not dying out so much as exploding in a crunch, in a pop. And then . . . then . . . the most absolute, final silence Jake had ever heard. So total, so desperate, not even the birds, not even the cicadas, not the breeze through the leaves—nothing dared violate it.

Until the woman in the window, her face so pallid she might have plastered it just that instant with stage makeup, shrieked, "Oh my God! Oh my God!"

That woke them all from their stupor. Oh, it woke them all right.

Jake, at the edge of the crowd, heard the first report as though it were a dream.

"His brains—oh my God!—his brains are spattered all over."

"Call the police!" someone else screamed. "Get an ambulance!"

Howie's mouth fell open. "Son of a bitch," he groaned. Something, finally, had reached him. Maybe now he'd confine his urinating to toilet bowls.

Jake didn't dare look. He switched the lead soldier from

**7**

one sweaty palm to the other. Maybe, he thought, the ambulance can put the brain together again. Maybe Chris will get up, after all, and walk right up to Howie and Gene and Stash and show them what being a man is all about.

But there was no stirring, of either Chris or anybody else. Except . . . except the rapid *click-clack* of shoes coming from the direction of Chris's apartment, where voices were whispering, "It's Mrs. Petropolous. Let her get through."

And all Jake could think of was, Don't let her see. Don't let her look. It'll kill her too.

It didn't, though. At least not then. Her eyes popped open; her tongue, fluttering, hung between her thin lips. A shriek welled up from the pit of her stomach and pierced the air so that the block reverberated with it. Then she fainted.

That's all. Next to the body of her son, the late Chris Petropolous, she fainted, with the hand she was using to clutch him drenched in blood that was already drying in the sunlight.

Jake ran home, oblivious to the crowd, to the still immobile Howie, up the stairs to the apartment, where it didn't make a difference anymore whether anyone was in the kitchen or not. He headed right for the bathroom where, in the nick of time, he raised the seat and vomited as though he had some deadly ailment.

# Chapter 2

He didn't need to or couldn't or didn't want to tell anyone about it. It just stayed there—the wail and the so-rapid falling and the crunch—so that on the Sunday afternoon almost four years later, when they were all—Mama and Papa and his three brothers who were much older than ten—listening to the Philco radio, and the trembling voice of the announcer blared out that Pearl Harbor had been attacked, it came back to him for just an instant. Chris Petropolous falling from that dizzying height, wailing. Because his daring to climb that pole in the first place and the call to arms addressed over the Philco radio to all the men of the land . . . well, they just seemed to belong together.

Jake knew that Chris Petropolous, had he still been living and old enough, would have answered that call and not been, like Jake, so afraid he wished the words on the radio were just a great big joke, a prank, that would be over the moment someone flicked the dial.

Only no one flicked the dial. And the prank didn't end. As in a dream, they—his brothers Max and Michael and Benjy—began to evaporate from the household. In the dark

9

of the morning, it always seemed like, each one came to the studio couch in the living room where he slept, crept up to him, and said, "So long, sport! You take care of yourself and Mama and Papa, and one day you'll be a man, too." It was hard to separate into days or weeks or months the distance between their departures; they seemed to blur together in a kind of crazy crisscrossing of hurried steps and whispers and tiny, choking sobs.

The sobs, Jake knew, belonged to Mama. That much he was certain of. Her pitch-black, short-cropped hair bobbed in and out of the murky silence of the dawn, trailing the choked sobs behind her in a perpetual lament. Her big sons actually *were* leaving now, not just going from her in the fear of her mind, but in actual, concrete, measurable fact. Going off to the war; invited to march off to the war in answer to individual letters from the United States government, addressed separately to them as though they were indeed men of the world.

And then, in that same blurring together of the crisscrossed, hurried steps and frantic whispers, the stars began to appear. The five-pointed blue stars, each one no larger than a silver dollar, began to appear on the white, satin, red-bordered flag that hung from a cord right in the center of the living-room window for everyone on Francisco Avenue to see. One star on top of the other, until there were three of them as vertical as that telephone pole, signifying to the world that here, on North Francisco Avenue, Chicago, Illinois, United States of America, in this very apartment, three men had gone to serve their country. To die, maybe. To perform courageous acts, maybe. To destroy the Axis powers, maybe, and ready the world for peace and freedom and love among men.

It was almost, for Jake, too much to bear, eyeing it each morning—winter and spring, summer and fall—from the bed in the prestigious bedroom he'd inherited from Benjy and Max, right off the living room. Lying there on his back with his head propped up by the pillow, in the stillness of the morning before anyone else was awake, he eyed it through the doorway, mesmerized by what it signified.

Oh, yes. He missed the three of them all right. There was no getting around that. Things were too quiet now—except for Mama's sobs. Papa quietly read those funny-looking letters when he was home from his one job making airplane propellers and his other job making tanks. They called the letters V-mail; they were photographed and reduced in size and sometimes had heavy black lines across certain words because the words gave away the names of secret locations.

Jake knew it wasn't the missing of the three that the stars signified most. What they signified most was that they—Max and Michael and Benjy—were old enough, men enough, to have been invited by the United States government, in special letters no less, to join in the salvation of the United States of America. While he, Jacob Ackerman, blood relative, was not man enough to do anything more than stare at the stars on that little white flag that stood for his brothers, and wonder, When? When, for godsakes, will they think I'm old enough? Will I ever be old enough?

Sometimes, lost in a reverie at school, he dreamed of wearing the boots or the khaki jackets or the caps all of them, in the photographs they sent home, wore. Not the medals. Oh, never the medals. That would have been too much, too presumptuous for a twelve-year-old to dream of. The boots and the other things seemed more reachable. Or, when he was startled out of a reverie by Miss Robertson or Miss Fagan and even the boots seemed preposterous, there was one other thing.

He could at least give up the lead soldiers. Bury them for

the duration in some dark recess of the apartment where they wouldn't always flash out at him and remind him of his childishness.

So one day, after school and alone now as usual, in his bedroom in a ritual nearly as elaborate as Mama's pre-Sabbath cleaning or her now less elaborate Saturday-night dinner preparations, he packed the lead soldiers in a cigar box he had coaxed from Herman, the corner candy-store owner; tamped them down with old newspaper; and sealed the box with a strip of bandage. His eyes moved from the star-studded flag in the living-room window to the cigar box and back. He shuddered with a strange fear that was mingled with an equally strange excitement and, to the emptiness of the room, muttered what amounted to an incantation: "That's it! It's over! Done with! There's no going back now!"

Just what exactly was over and done with that couldn't be gone back to ever, he didn't know. All he knew was that in it, somewhere, was that flag and that wailing, fading into the blue sky above the falling body that now, right at this moment, if it hadn't fallen, would have been Chris Petropolous.

He buried the cigar box in the farthest, deepest recess of the bedroom closet, beneath those books Papa referred to, though not very often anymore, as the *Gemara,* the commentaries. Even under the stack of records Papa sometimes said contained the most beautiful voice he'd ever heard: the voice of Cantor Yossele Rosenblatt.

And then he stood back, his hands tingling with fear and excitement, and yelled out loud enough for Mama, cutting her noodles in the kitchen, to hear, "I'm going to get a job. Tomorrow after school I'm going to look for a job."

That was, of course, one way to draw attention to himself in an apartment where, for months now—maybe even years, for all he could remember—all attention was riveted on the three, not lead but living, soldiers of the family.

It was that, all right. But it must have been more, too.

It had to be the flag . . . and Chris as well that made him know a job was the next step.

And all the next day, through the air-raid and fire-drill practices, through arithmetic, through science, he plotted his course.

"The cube root of twenty-seven, Jacob Ackerman, is three. Why can't you figure that out, for goodness' sakes?"

Maybe so. Maybe that's what twenty-seven's cube root was. But there was no finding of jobs in cube roots, of twenty-seven or any other number.

So Jake smiled abashedly back at Mrs. Devine to keep her from noticing that his mind wasn't exactly on cube roots, and mumbled something that sounded like "Sorry, ma'am," and prayed she'd get the hint and move on, maybe to Herschel Levin or Gloria Lombardi, who were always good at being down-to-earth and ready with right answers, and just leave him alone to continue the plotting, the planning.

She did, bless her! With a slow, disappointed shake of the head that said as much as any number of words she might instead have uttered about what a shame it was, in a world so full of troubles, that otherwise good kids couldn't be gotten to do their homework.

And now he was free to pretend to be into the arithmetic book while really trying to picture, to recall, every storefront, every restaurant, every business along the lengths of Division Street and California Avenue. They weren't great lengths he had to contend with. California between North Avenue and, where the school was, Augusta Boulevard. Division Street between Sacramento on the west and Western on the east.

Sometimes Howie and Gene and Stash, on the few occasions when they deigned to acknowledge his existence, mocked him for that limited universe of his, for being a mama's boy.

It hurt. Oh boy, did it ever hurt—being called a mama's boy right in the middle of the war to end fascism and totalitarianism.

But that was another matter. Right now, the problem was to remember as exactly as possible what stores, what restaurants, what businesses were where.

And worse than that, how to work up the guts to go into one of them or all of them and say, "Have you got a job for a twelve-year-old? I can do anything!"

Like hell he could! Sure, he could sweep floors. Mama had seen to that. And he could mold clay hills, really neat ones with crags and crevices and ridges, so that they almost looked real, and take the lead brigade up one side—chivalrous, brave, courageous, unafraid of death—while forcing the lead brigade on the other side down in inglorious humiliation.

He could sure do that to perfection.

But that didn't help decide where to go first. Whether to Weinberg's Grocery Store, where Max had once worked for three dollars a week until someone jumped him one night after closing and beat his face to a pulp, just to get the three dollars out of his pocket.

A possibility, but not a good one. Decidedly not a good one. Mrs. Weinberg was too bossy and prettied-up for anyone to be able to stand her for more than thirty minutes at a time, let alone a whole afternoon and part of the evening after school.

Meanwhile, the class trooped from arithmetic to Room 105, where Mr. Swiatek promised that the film on amoebas was really going to be informative, but where, instead, in the heavy darkness behind the black window shades, Jake was free, with his eyes half-closed, to study the whole problem carefully.

Being a busboy in a place like Demetrius' Cafe just had no appeal. Big deal! Carting trays and dishes back and forth between the five tables and kitchen.

On the other hand, ushering at the Vision, now that had a few real advantages. Especially on the weekends, when they ran the Buck Rogers serials. An usher wouldn't have to worry about whether or not his folks could spare a quarter for the movie in order to keep up with Buck's adventures with The Terrible Ming.

Better yet would be a job soda-jerking at Jack's. Forget the fact that the soda jerk could probably have as many malts and shakes and banana splits as he wanted. A plus, definitely. But not nearly as important as the power he'd have winning a few friends here and there with, say, at first, a surreptitious scoop of ice cream, escalating to, a little later, the special of the house, a triple-rich root beer float. A few friends here and there, that wasn't a thing to be knocked.

Of course, too, there was Rosenberg's Deli. Christ, but the corned beef always smelled great all the way out on the street! Like a magnet it pulled, making a person wish he had all the money in the world and needed only the taste for it, the incredible craving, to go in there and walk right up and say, "A hot, lean corned beef on rye to go, with a large chocolate phosphate and extra green pickles . . . please." The *please,* obviously, was important, so as not to leave anyone with the impression that having all the money in the world gave you certain inalienable rights, including the right to be pompous.

The trouble was, the film on amoebas didn't last nearly

long enough. And when Mr. Swiatek jerked the window-shade cords so that the shades swished up to the top of the windows and came to an abrupt dead end with a *whack,* Jake wasn't any more certain about where and how to begin than he'd been when he'd gotten up that morning and studied the three-starred flag. His head buzzed with questions, with doubts, with perplexities and confusions so rampant, he didn't even realize the bell had rung and that the fingers digging into his shoulder belonged to Howie Woscowicz.

"See you outside, Ackerman," he said, sneering pretty much the same way he had when he'd sat atop the overturned litter basket in the park and discovered toilets weren't the only things one could urinate into.

Jake tried at first to ease out of the grip, to pretend it didn't mean what it seemed to.

But then, when he turned fully around and saw Gene and Stash standing there too, he stopped.

Some grips are too firm to ease out from under.

So he looked Howie as straight in the eye as he could—as straight as, maybe, Chris might have, or Max or Michael or Benjy were probably doing right that minute facing some German solider in North Africa or somewhere else—and stammered, "If you say so, Howie."

And for the next half hour, looking for a job wasn't terribly important.

Survival was.

# Chapter 3

Slowly, thoughtfully, he stacked his books together and kept one eye on the three of them as they walked cockily towards the exit.

Well, there were two ways—that's all—to handle it.

There was the diplomatic way: mild-mannered, deferential, a smidgen of—not a lot, but just enough—cowering to show them he'd learned that a little urinating now and then goes a long way.

Jake shifted his books from under one arm to under the other, still eyeing the three swaggering figures, who didn't even need to glance back over their shoulders to check to see if he were following, so certain were they of the power of the shadows they cast.

It was irksome, that's what it was. All that certainty, all that swagger.

Which led Jake to wonder about the other, the second way. *That* sent shudders through him even as he thought about it. Taking on all three of them at once wasn't, after all, quite the same as getting a job. A job, at least, took time: time to adjust, to get used to. It didn't happen all of a sudden, with a couple of solid thwacks to the head or gut and then total oblivion.

But there was something to be said for the latter approach anyway. What it had going for it were the three-starred flag and Chris Petropolous.

So as he neared the exit, Jake sucked in the deepest breath he'd ever in his whole life sucked in, and girded up his loins by tightening his belt another one or two notches, and gritted his teeth and mumbled, "This is for you, Max, and you, Michael, and you, Benjy. And . . . and . . . Chris, you'd be proud, too. They're just guys, right? What's the worst they can do? Kill me?"

That was a thought, all right. But there wasn't time to think it through to its conclusion, for there they were, the three of them, with Howie in the forefront, smirking, his fists clenched and resting on his hips.

Jake lowered his books to the ground, not in any kind of premeditated way, as though he'd really thought about the consequences of getting whacked around, but instinctively, like a cornered cat that somehow knows enough to arch its back when things are about to start getting tight.

He didn't yet dare raise his eyes to meet theirs. Instead, he searched the gravel of the school yard, hoping, maybe, to find a mislaid rabbit's foot or a four-leaf clover or God-only-knows-what.

Then the word rang out. Oh, did the word ring out! Like the huge clapper of a huge bell in a sealed-in steeple, the word assailed the ears so, they hurt with a pounding, throbbing, stabbing hurt that made Jake's head explode in splinters of blood that pierced every part of him.

"KIKE!" Howie bellowed, still smirking, still snug in the comfort of his station in life.

Gene and Stash, behind him, sneered the way followers of

powerful leaders do when they are secure in the leader's shadow.

It wasn't just a word now. Maybe, at an earlier time, before Chris, before the announcement over the Philco radio and the dark dawn disappearances of his brothers—maybe before all that, it would only have been a word.

But now, in the middle of the school yard with a crowd already forming a circle around the imminent battle, it was as much a call to arms as the president's earlier call to arms had been.

A circle exactly like the circle around the telephone pole. Not close in, not tight. Who needs to touch destiny where, with all the dangers destiny is fraught with, contamination is possible, is likely?

No! The crowd of blurred faces held back, gave room.

The faces were all the same to Jake, who saw them spinning as he moved his head from side to side through blood-splintered eyes. Only, finally, his eyes had to come to rest on Howie. And that wasn't the same. It wasn't any longer that awesome, fearful visage hovering over the wood-bottomed litter container in Humboldt Park. Now it was only a thin-lipped, smirky countenance that needed to be taught something—that needed to be taught that you don't go and fool around with all the things a person's brothers stand for.

A strange, new energy surged through Jake's body. He didn't know if the feeling was real or not. He didn't care anymore. If it was real, he'd find out soon enough. If it wasn't, he'd find that out soon enough, too.

He raced up to the ogre of Francisco Avenue, his arms flailing wildly about, enraged at having to be put to the test this soon, so much before he'd planned for it. Before getting a job, before being old enough to be eligible to receive his own special invitation from the United States government.

Laughable, that's what it was. Like a kid swatting some poor, blue-tailed fly. Howie just straight-armed him, that's all. He smirked that arrogant smirk of his. Not all the flailing in the world would have allowed Jake to get within two, three inches of his body.

But Jake flailed anyway, once or twice barely managing to fingertip Howie's arm.

So what that Gene and Stash were practically hysterical now? "Cmon, kike. You better knock old Howie out or we're going to piss on you again."

So what that the blurred faces in the crowd emitted these shrieks as thunderous nearly as a clapping bell in a sealed-in steeple?

Everybody's got to die—once.

Jake struck out at the ogre again and again, blindly, aimlessly, furiously, and all the pent-up horror of the crash from the telephone pole and the diminishment of the size of his family brought on by the war coalesced in a single, simple desire: not to be humiliated. To, at the very least, come away from it all with wounds and bruises sufficient to proclaim to the world: "I'm not scared! Maybe I'm not a man, but at least I'm not scared either."

Howie's punches told. Did they ever tell! Each one—to the head, to the gut, to the arm—sent Jake reeling, spinning, throbbing, quaking so much with pain he could scarcely stand straight anymore.

One of them caught him right in the eye. He tried, he wanted to sidestep it the second he saw it coming, but his legs gave out on him right then and there, and there was nothing to do but accept it, like some sort of unexpected gift one ought to be grateful for. And when it landed, fitted into the socket of his eye, the way a hand might fit into a glove, it

**20**

smarted so, it tingled so, it crushed so much color into the eye at once, Jake nearly forgot where he was. Maybe, in fact, he wasn't anywhere. Maybe it was one of those dreams where you float along the curve of a rainbow and get so caught up in the loveliness of the color you forget you're looking for the pot of gold at the end.

Maybe.

But then again, maybe not. Because if it were a dream, what the hell were Gene and Stash doing in it, grabbing him around the neck now, burning the goddamned skin off him? And why the hell was there all that laughing? Like in an echo chamber where, no matter how hard he tried to close his ears, the word *kike* rumbled in on him—Jesus!—just like a high-speed train racing downhill.

Until, that is, his legs crumbled under him like a couple of matchsticks.

Then everything stopped. Suddenly. Abruptly. Completely. All at once. *P-L-O-M-B! C-R-U-N-C-H!*

The silence was overwhelming. It covered Jake as much as the dust and gravel he lay in. Only the silence pained more, dug in more deeply. Stung and ached nearly as much as the punches and the burning neck.

He didn't dare move. He didn't dare look up out of the dust and gravel he lay in to find out why, suddenly, it had grown so quiet and dark.

He just lay there, subtly aware that the nail on his forefinger was split right down the middle, oozing blood—not nearly as red or profuse as Chris's blood or even, maybe, the blood that right at that second, on totally different battle-fields, might be oozing from Max's or Michael's or Benjy's fingers or God-knows-where-else.

Blood! His own Medal of Honor. Staring at it, hypnotized by the trickling, rippling red line coursing down from the split fingernail, he could almost—not completely—imagine himself being approached by some general or admiral and being called forward from out of the ranks of men of courage to be presented with his very own award.

But not completely. He couldn't—didn't have time to really get the picture set against the background of his half-shut eyes. The shuffling, scratching of feet on the school yard gravel interfered. No other noise. Just the scratching of feet on the gravel.

He squinted through eyes that would have preferred being shut off from the outside world.

The crowd—the blurred legs and feet, it seemed every single body in Lafayette School—was receding, ebbing away, aghast, petrified at the object, which is what Jake thought of himself as being, so still now someone could have easily mistaken him for a rock or something—prostrate on the gray gravel.

Why, after all, should *they* want to stare defeat in the face? Recognize, maybe, that it's easier to fall than to rise? It was hard enough for him to. They didn't need to.

Only the arrogant, haughty, victorious, pulled-back shoulders of Howie, Gene, and Stash remained in sight. Swaggering still, the bosses of Francisco Avenue, tenured now more than ever, with at least two scalps under their belts—Jake's and Chris's.

Well, one day—who knew?—their scalps would be hanging from someone else's belt.

Jake waited, his heart pounding less fiercely now, the meaning of it all somewhat clearer in his head.

The job! That's what he thought. I've got to get a darn job.

He hauled himself up from the gravel, prickling all over from the sharp edges and ridges of the gravel he'd been lying on, and dusted himself off.

The humiliation of facing everyone tomorrow was still a thing to be contended with, but there wasn't time for that. Afternoon shadows were already beginning to extend across the school yard. If he was to get a job and not have to go through one more night of staring shamefully at those three stars on the satin flag hanging in the living-room window, he had to put the humiliation out of his head, at least for now.

Now what he had to do was go up and down the lengths of Division and California, knocking from door to door and hoping no one would turn him away just because of the stinging right eye and the bleeding fingernail.

# Chapter 4

It seemed as though most of them did turn him away.

Mrs. Weinberg, heavily mascaraed, scarcely looked up from the bill she was totaling on a customer's grocery bag. She wet the pencil tip in her mouth every other second and mumbled the prices as she wrote them down, adding little gibes here and there about the way the war was making the cost of food skyrocket; it wasn't her fault.

Jake stood behind the customer, fidgeting timidly, wishing Mr. Weinberg wasn't in the back stockpiling black-market— the word in the neighborhood had it—cans of salmon. It would have been easier to beg, plead for a job from the man of the house.

He waited, his face twisted away from Mrs. Weinberg enough to keep the searing, tormenting eye out of sight. If she were going to turn him down, it couldn't, it musn't be for that—because he'd gotten a black eye from Howie.

Finally she spoke up, in that sharp-edged voice of hers he'd come to know by heart from all the times he'd been forced to hear it when Mama had sent him in for a box of this or a pound of that.

"Max?" Mrs. Weinberg said. "So what do you hear from Max? Such a worker! Such a young man! Your mother's blessed, let me tell you, to have a son like that."

Jake put on the very best smile it was possible for someone remembering how good a son Max was to put on.

"He's fine, ma'am," he said. For a moment he'd toyed with the idea of calling her by name. But the intimacy of it seemed too tactless under the circumstances. Business was business. This wasn't the time to be intimate.

A long, painful silence ensued while she packed the customer's grocery bag and he fidgeted, rehearsing in his head the right words to use, the right pose to assume. For the first time since the school yard, his finger ached. But he didn't dare tend to it now. Not in front of her, where the slightest wrong move might diminish his chances.

"What's your mother want today, eh?" Mrs. Weinberg said when the customer picked up her bag and left.

The moment of truth was at hand. Jake trembled.

He put the smile back on and groped stupidly for a way to get into it, for a way to say, "The flag in the window bothers me a lot. A job will make the pain easier."

What came out was quite different. So different, so bold, so . . . so self-confident, it shocked him to hear it.

"It's not my mother," he said. "It's me. I want a job."

The effort of saying it left him feeling hollow, disembodied. It was like . . . well, it was like he hadn't said it at all. Some other kid—his size, his build—had said it. And he, Jacob Ackerman, had simply hovered above it all and overheard it.

She turned her mascaraed, emotionless face to him and with the keen edge of her voice made her decision unequivocably. "No," she said. "Times are bad. Who can afford help?"

25

Jake backed away, the bad side of his face still shadowed from her view.

Times are bad for everyone, Mrs. Weinberg, he thought. But that's not what he said. What he said now was, "I understand, ma'am."

The hell he did! He didn't understand anything, except that if you couldn't get a job at twelve, when the hell were you supposed to get it?

There he was, back on Division Street, in square one all over again. He put the split fingernail to his mouth to suck off some of the hurt, to give himself time to think.

He turned left, toward Demetrius' Cafe and the Vision Theater, but the knot inside him had grown so big, he shuddered just at the thought of being tossed out on his ear again.

Anyway, who wanted to be a busboy, an usher? And what if the corned beef smelled so good outside Rosenberg's? Or if a person could have tons of friends just by dishing out free ice cream and floats at Jack's?

Standing there at the intersection of Division and California—the crossroads into and out of the only world he knew, the world of Humboldt Park—he dug into his pocket, the bad finger bent back in gingerly protection, and dragged out a penny. In the hot afternoon sun, he stood there motionless, mindless of the people passing, and studied the penny a good long while.

It was the only one he had left.

But there was no question about it! A penny's worth of sunflower seeds went a long way toward clearing the head. And, if he needed anything now, it was a clear head, without all the buzzing and ringing of Howie's fist in it, in order to get that job, in order not to have to go back home exactly the way he'd left in the morning.

He walked to the glass-domed sunflower-seed machine

shackled to the wall of Arnie's Liquor Store, dropped the penny in the slot, gave the handle a good solid twist to the right, and let the sunflower seeds cascade out of the door into the palm of his hand.

They were good.

They were awfully good. The salt bit into his tongue and stung his lips so that he had to lick them. The cool aftertaste of his tongue eased the burning until he slid another seed between his teeth, cracked the shell, and the burning, stinging began once more.

Still they were good. They sharpened his senses; woke him up to what still lay ahead, to what he still had to do.

He turned south on California, sucking, crunching, chewing the seeds, trying to ignore the stabbing pain in his eye, glancing to either side of the street, hoping a thing to do would come into his mind. A kind of magic sign that could point out to him just the right place to go where, with no great effort, a job, *the* job, would be waiting for him.

A breeze blew softly through the silver maples, and a streetcar clanged its way in the distance. People were already coming home from work, leaping from the rear platform of the streetcar onto the cobblestone area of the tracks, their faces weary from work, their legs buckling from the ride.

Jake walked, paused, tried to build up the courage it would take to make that first move.

In a few short steps, he had reached Crystal Square.

The street sign startled him.

Something in the deepest part of him tried to push its way to his brain, tried to rush forward, to erupt out of him into consciousness. Someone, somebody, had once said something about Crystal Square. But he couldn't put his finger on who or what it was.

For no special reason—except maybe because of the way

27

the sun was hitting it and giving it an eerie, almost Draculan cast—the long green opaque window of the first building he came to past the alley brought him to an abrupt halt. There were scratches in it. Letters, worn jagged with time, announced at the top of the window that the building was the site of GOLD, INC. But that, in itself, wasn't enough to cause the intrigue, the compelling urge that made him lean into the glass and, with his hands cupped around his eyes, peer intently into each scratch to discover what secret the forbidding green window was designed to veil from the outside world.

There were noises, too.

Garbled voices, sometimes interspersed with laughter, and sounding vaguely as though they belonged to kids his own age.

And there was the steady, low hum of machines.

And a smell that seemed, in fact, to be seeping through the opaque window itself. A smell unlike any Jake had ever smelled before. Sweet, warm—but not the sort that would come from a kitchen. He couldn't exactly place it, give a name to it, as it filled his nostrils. But he knew right away it was the kind of smell a person could live with if he had to.

It was then—sucking in the smell, trying to evaluate it—that the memory came to him, the memory that had eluded him at the sight of the street sign. GOLD, INC.—Max had once said something about the place and the desk pads they made there. In fun, as a joke, nearly in ridicule. Jake remembered it now: "The shop on Crystal Square. Gold—the old man who runs the place—uses kids there. Can you believe that? Uses kids to take the place of men."

That's what came back now. Max's saying that once, before Pearl Harbor, before Chris's fall from the pole, before all of them disappeared and left him alone.

It was all Jake needed.

He went to the green, opaque glass door, raised his good hand to knock, held it suspended in the air for a second, then abruptly decided to throw caution to the wind.

"The hell with it!" he muttered. "Might as well just go right in."

Which is exactly how he met Harry Katz, first and, seconds later, old man Gold himself.

# Chapter 5

He just about knocked the load of cardboard right out of Harry Katz's arms with that swinging-in of the glass door.

"Damn!" Harry yelled. "Why don't you watch where you're going?"

A kid so tall, with cheekbones and nose so sharply chiseled, he could easily be fourteen or fifteen.

"Sorry," Jake said, meaning it and realizing, in the kind of flash that comes to a person without reason but stays forever, that this was someone he might be knowing for a long time. "Didn't mean it."

Harry, struggling to balance the pile of cardboard in arms that rippled with enviable muscularity, grimaced. "Okay," he said. "It's okay."

And he fumbled his way out of reach of the door and Jake, towards a darkened hallway to the right, and disappeared.

Leaving Jake naked, in the open, inside the shop, surrounded by a cacophony of voices and droning machines, and the smell, that smell that was sweet and warm. Alone. Standing there isolated in the doorway, the long, opaque green window to his left, and a cluttered, scratched mahogany desk to his right, just beyond the shadowed hallway where Harry Katz had disappeared with the stack of cardboard. Conscious of the burning, raging eye. Uncertain, now that he was actually inside, of how to begin, of how to say, "Well, there was Chris first of all, and then the war, and finally Max and Michael and Benjy, and only now, practically this very minute, Howie Woscowicz."

It wasn't at all like facing Mrs. Weinberg at the grocery store. She . . . well, he knew her from before. It was easier asking for a job from someone you knew.

But this was foreign territory. This was practically the end of the universe. This was like being an army scout behind enemy lines.

A voice—deep, gravelly, unequivocably certain of itself—bellowed out from the farthest corner of the wall where the desk stood.

"So? What's the matter? The cat got your tongue?"

Jake's eyes moved cautiously to the corner. A man shaped like a keg, with a head so bald the overhead light made it glisten, stood there. Short and thick-jowled, he absolutely commanded attention.

Jake trembled forward, trying to keep his mind off the two rows of sneering, inquisitive eyes and lips that lined the long table off to the left. Muted, those faces were testing him, measuring him in their silence for his right to belong among them.

He caught them in the corner of his good eye, testing them too but not nearly as intently as they him. There wasn't time for more than a quick thought: Damn, they look older than me!

The old keg wasn't being helpful. His steely gray eyes looked as though he was prepared to wait forever—or until Jake spoke up, whichever came first.

The vacuum was unbearable.

Jake stammered his way right into it, to fill it up before it smothered him.

"Do you need . . . er, are you in need of . . . ah. I'm looking for a . . . are you hiring anybody today?"

It was so god-awful dumb, when the echo of it came back to him, the only thing Jake could be glad of was that he'd whispered it out of earshot of all the heads along the table.

The old man's steely gray eyes didn't flutter once. If they'd moved at all, it might have been enough to send Jake hightailing it right back onto Crystal Square. They just locked him in a fierce iron grip from which he couldn't have struggled free even if he had wanted to.

"That's the way you ask a person for a job?" the old man croaked. "What's the matter? You don't have a name?"

The blood rushed to Jake's face, erasing the pain of the eye, of Howie, of the throbbing fingernail.

"Jake Ackerman," he said at last. He would have added "sir" except that it seemed inappropriate addressed to a lump of a man whose thick, twisted lips were already shaping, preparing to croak still another humiliation at him.

"How old are you, kid?" the man said. His lips turned up at the corners in a faint smile; the eyes warmed up to a pastel gray.

Now, for the first time, the man moved, and Jake detected a limp, a heaviness on one side of the man's body that compensated for a left leg shorter by an inch or two than the right.

The defect, strangely enough, pleased Jake. Not that he wished the old man any harm. Not that at all. It simply put the two of them on a more equal basis; made it easier to answer the question honestly.

"Twelve," he whispered. He was tempted to explain how

a person's actual age wasn't nearly as important as how old he felt.

But it was too late for that, because the questions kept coming.

"You ever work before, eh? You responsible? I can't have loafers around here! Here, we work, do you understand?"

All Jake could think to do—staring at the hardened globules of glue on the man's green apron, and wondering if the warm, sweet, pervasive smell belonged to the glue—was nod.

He kept nodding until it hit him that the barrage of questions implied its own answer.

He's going to hire me, for Chrissakes!

The pummeling in the school yard hadn't been for nothing. Neither had Chris's fall or the war.

He was going to be given a chance to make up for all that.

"Katz!" the old man bellowed. "Bring an apron for the new boy."

Harry Katz, with his chiseled features, strutted towards them to the hum of the machines, thrust a folded green apron into Jake's hands, and disappeared. He didn't utter a word. No one else in the shop uttered a word.

Except the old man, whom Jake now guessed to be Mr. Gold himself. He commanded. "Come on, Jake Ackerman," he said. "Let's see what kind of worker you are."

He limped to the shadowed rear of the shop and Jake, robot-like, followed.

# Chapter 6

So it was, at almost 4:30 P.M. exactly, on that late April afternoon in 1943, that Jake, trailing behind the limping, keg-shaped, bald-headed Izzie Gold, began the trek that would lead right into the Bar Mitzvahs and Harry Katz.

With no hint, with no foreshadowing at all, keeping his eye on the rise and fall of old man Gold's lopsided body as it led the way, Jake had no way of knowing that in that man's limp lay a world full of knowledge that he, Jake, could learn from.

Knowledge, for instance, of pain, with Izzie Gold stiffening in a spasm that cut across his body from the left hip to the right shoulder as he led Jake to the rear.

It lasted only a moment. Just long enough for the spasm to pass.

But Jake already knew from the way the back convulsed for that brief moment that the old man wasn't going to let pain keep him from his work.

Jake recorded the moment somewhere deep in his head.

They reached the shadowed recess of the windowless back

room when the old man suddenly swung on the longer of his two legs and faced Jake.

Vestiges of the pain creased the old man's jowled face, especially the thick lips, where the pale imprint of teeth marks was still visible.

Chris Petropolous's lips might have made the same mark. But Jake would never know, not having had the courage to peer in closely at Chris's body as it lay crumpled at the foot of the telephone pole.

"You'll emboss!" was all Izzie Gold said.

His spatulate finger pointed to an iron machine belching flame in the center of the tiny room that otherwise was eerie and dark.

Jake shuddered. Whatever the hell did that mean? How could a person "emboss" if he didn't even know what it meant?

But the finger wasn't interested in questions. Jake's eyes followed the finger to where the bluish yellow tufts of flame hissed out of the holes in infernal insistence.

"Yes sir," he whispered. It was awfully hard to say anything more without inviting Izzie Gold's displeasure.

Jake simply obeyed, that's all.

He lifted himself up on a stool, so that now he sat facing the tongues of flame that licked at the edges of the holes. For the first time, he felt it—the thing which, like the smell of the glue, seemed to capture everything the shop stood for—the fierce heat shooting out of the machine. It enveloped him. It smothered him.

God! he thought. What the hell am I doing here? I ought to be home with my toy soldiers.

Already the sweat dripped from his forehead.

He wanted to take a swipe at it, to wipe it away.

But the steely eyes were still on him and he didn't dare.

"Take this," old man Gold said. He handed Jake a sheet of gold as thin as gossamer that sparkled in the flames.

Jake took it in his trembling fingers. What else was there to do? The shiny side of the sheet of gold was so smooth it began to slide through his fingers. He had to focus hard on what he was doing just to cling to it.

"It's all right," old man Gold said. "You got to get used to it, the way it slips and slides. There's a way."

Jake turned slowly to look into old man Gold's eyes. In the light of the flames, they had suddenly become softer, more lenient. The pain, too, had passed from the old man's lips so that now the lips were freer somehow, better able to form words.

"Like this?" Jake said, holding the four-by-five sheet with his thumb on the dull, rough side and his forefinger pressing down on the shiny side.

"Good!" old man Gold said. "Now I show you how to emboss."

And the mysterious word slowly took on meaning as Gold lifted Jake's free arm—not fully but at the bend of the elbow—steered it toward the lever at the side of the machine, and made Jake's hand take hold of the lever and raise it up and down so that it raised and lowered the flame-licked plate.

"It's called a die," Izzie Gold said, pointing to the underside of the iron plate where an intricately tooled block of metal was fastened. When the lever brought the iron plate down to eye level, the block of metal touched the gold leaf and left a gold imprint on a piece of leather—a scroll fine and even.

Jake gasped. Geez, he thought, that's something.

Old man Gold's spatulate fingers still gripped Jake's forearm, but now he smiled at his new employee as well.

"Take your time and do it right, Ackerman," he said. "And everything will be something. Do you understand? That's all that counts: making everything into something."

Jake nodded, but without understanding. He lifted, one after the other, the strips of leather Gold had pointed out to him in the pile to the left of the machine, placed them under the die with the gold leaf on top, and brought the lever down—quickly, sharply—to make the scrolled imprint.

Old man Gold picked up each finished strip of leather and inspected it, scrutinized it in the light of the flames.

"Messy" is all he said as he traced the outline of the scroll on the leather with his jagged-nailed fingertip. The gold had spread beyond the outline of the scroll. That, Jake understood, was what made the imprint messy. "Crap like this, any kid can do. You want to work for me, you emboss clean, sharp. Do you understand?"

There was all this understanding to do. It made Jake sweat profusely. But he couldn't give up.

So he kept on nodding. He kept on trying. And he began to forget the clot of blood on his finger and the throbbing eye.

Until, on the fifteenth or sixteenth piece of leather, old man Gold finally said, "Better."

That's all. Just "Better." Without another word, leaving Jake to fend for himself, he turned his back and left the back room. Just moved away, like a shadow that disappears with a waning sun.

Jake was all alone, staring into the fascinating, frightening dance of the flames, with nothing left to do to keep himself from crying like a baby but emboss.

# Chapter 7

He didn't know how he got through the next hour or so. It seemed longer than all the other years of his life put together.

The sweat trickled down his forehead and into his eyes, but with the image of the old man so powerfully a part of the place, Jake didn't, couldn't, bring himself to wipe the sweat away.

He kept on embossing—robot-like almost—despite the discomfort, despite the sweat that, having dripped down his neck, now coursed its way under his shirt to his chest, to his belly.

He wanted to scream, to call quits to the whole damned thing; it wasn't worth it. Not all the stars, all the battles, all the Howie Woscowiczes in the world were worth it.

Up went the lever; down went the lever. The machine, with a life of its own, hissed out its flames, its blue flames with their yellow or orange centers tonguing out, flicking out at him, chiding him, tantalizing him, egging him on in a test of wills to see who could last longer.

Jake wouldn't give in.

The old man had said "Better," hadn't he? And the opposite of *better* was *messy*. That much Jake already knew. The old man hadn't been exactly subtle. Avoid messy, go for better.

Somehow the battle between messy and better had something to do with taking your time, doing a thing right, and making everything into something.

He felt it as, with each imprinted strip of leather, he ran his fingertips over the scrolls indented on the surface of the leather, to see if the gold had spread out beyond the imprints.

On some of the strips of leather, the gold had.

Jake felt absolutely shitty when it did.

He didn't know what to do, though: whether to just put the messy strip in the pile with the better ones or call out, from that deep, dark recess at the rear of the shop, to Mr. Gold and say, "Hey, I goofed. I did a messy one. Help me."

If he did the wrong thing, why, the old man could race (limp?) back there, grab him by an arm, and kick him the hell out of there right back onto the street to face Howie and Gene and Stash again, no different from before.

So he played it safe. He stuffed the messy strips into his pocket. And when the number of messy strips rose indecently to seven, eight, ten, twelve, he started stuffing the other pocket.

Maybe, the thought crossed Jake's mind, maybe Max had been right, way back in that time before the war. Maybe old man Gold hired kids to do men's work. Men didn't stuff spoiled strips of embossed leather into their pockets, did they? Men made everything into something.

By the time it neared six and he was itching to get out, to go home and pour everything out to Mama—the eye, the finger, the job—Jake was numb.

He twisted on the stool. He spit on his finger and jabbed at the iron plate of the embossing machine to see just how hot the damned thing really was.

The spit on his finger sizzled. The machine was pretty damned hot.

Someone should come—maybe Mr. Gold, maybe Katz with the chiseled-out cheekbones and sharp nose—and tell him what the hell to do now. It was getting late.

But nobody did.

They'd forgotten him, for pete's sake, in this coffin of a room where, in the eerie light of the flames, he could barely, only barely, make out the shadows of rolls of paper or leather or God-only-knows-what—dancing along the walls, peeled and cracked and—could it be?—amok with scurrying roaches or spiders.

He unstuck his sweaty rear from the stool and took a few—not many, not enough to cause a rustle and send the whole horde of them from the front of the shop to investigate—steps around the table just to check things out. Like the cardboard box the sheets of gold leaf came from, just behind the embossing machine, which he fingered and then, out of curiosity, took some sheets out of. And soon the temptation was so strong, he didn't have the strength to turn away until he'd snatched one, like a thief in the night, and smushed it into his pocket, along with the spoiled strips of leather.

Well, it wasn't his fault, was it? The least someone could do was come get him, tell him it was time—which it was—to go home.

That one single sheet of gold, along with the strips of leather, burned in his pocket as fiercely as the machine itself.

And Jake hated himself for it, for the weakness of it, for not having enough strength or willpower or whatever to do the right thing.

He was beside himself now. Too numb to sit; afraid, with those things scurrying about on the walls, to stand.

Was it any wonder the government of the United States of America hadn't sent him, as it had Max and Michael and Benjy, a special invitation to join in the fight against the Axis powers?

He worked the lever up and down furiously now, just for something to do, stamping out one leather strip after another, trying the best way he could to make them come out halfway decent, but no longer really caring.

That's when—half-awake, half-asleep—he heard it for the first time. The music. Long-haired, squeaky, cymbal-clashing music with, every now and then, a voice—no, voices—talking, singing. Jake didn't know which—whether a man's voice, so high-pitched it seemed like a girl's, or a woman's voice, so deep and resonant it could have been mistaken for a man's—was talking or singing or what.

It didn't fit, that's all. It didn't belong in the shop; that was Jake's first impression. "Damn," he muttered. "What the hell's going on?"

He folded his hands on his lap; he plucked at the green apron to raise it above the pockets stuffed with ruined strips of leather, to cover up his crimes.

But it didn't work.

And now there wasn't time to do anything about it.

Because now old man Gold lumbered in, the keg of his body tilting precariously with each heavy-footed step so that Jake knew the body tilted long before he saw it, from the thump of one foot, followed by the shuffle of the other, longer one.

Jake stared harder into the flame, his face taut and frightened. He gripped the embossing lever so tightly his fingers hurt.

He pressed his knees together to hide the evidence of his crimes.

Old man Gold simply said, "Recitative. A recitative from *La Bohème*."

Not in those imperious, teeth-clenched tones of two hours ago, when Jake first crossed the threshold into the green universe of the shop, but in the softer, gentler tone of the word *better,* when Jake had finally produced an embossed strip that wasn't messy. Caressing almost, like the stroke of a brush across a canvas.

Jake stopped fidgeting on the stool. Still, *recitative,* like the long-haired music itself, didn't seem to fit.

"Yes sir," Jake mumbled. He didn't turn to face the man. He just wished he'd say, "Go home now. Come back tomorrow."

When the sound of his own voice died out and there was—except for the drone of the music—this prolonged stillness, it occurred to Jake: The two of them, he and Mr. Gold, were all alone in the shop. Everyone else had gone home already.

The strangest, most peculiar tight feeling came over him, like being shut up in a prisoner-of-war cell with neither air nor light nor food.

Jake counted backward to himself. One thousand, nine hundred ninety-nine, nine hundred ninety-eight, nine hundred ninety-seven. That's what prisoners of war did. To save themselves from going crazy.

Old man Gold said, "When I first came to this country, when I lived in New York, every time Caruso sang at the Metropolitan Opera, I went. Do you hear?"

Jake heard. "Yes, sir," he mumbled. He began fidgeting again, lifting his rear from the stool just enough—not obviously, of course—to relieve the itch from all that goddamned sweat pooling in the crack.

"And when Caruso sang the part of Rudolfo, ach! It was something. Such beauty! Such a voice!"

Jake stifled a yawn. Not out of boredom. Not out of tedium. Out of just plain being tired.

"So what's a recita—— whatever you said?" he wanted to ask. "I mean, do you want me to come back tomorrow? Am I getting paid? Or what?"

But he didn't ask. How could he? He had scarcely enough energy left to keep up a smile.

So that when old man Gold, waking up from whatever reverie he'd been in, started checking the strips, Jake trembled.

The moment of truth was at hand.

The Day of Judgment had arrived.

God was about to deliver up His verdict.

And when he did, the tone of voice had changed again. Imperious once more. Authoritative. Commanding.

"You got a social security number?" old man Gold asked.

Jake hadn't even thought about that. He shook his head.

"Get one," old man Gold said.

Jake nodded, although he hadn't the slightest notion of how or where he was supposed to do that.

"Every day," old man Gold said. "You come in every day after school and emboss."

At last. Finally. Jesus Christ! It was done. He had a job and the old man hadn't even said, "You're hired."

Jake started to get up. Old man Gold touched his arm, nudged him really, and said, "Forty-five cents an hour you get to start. You work out, I'll give you more. You understand?"

Oh, Jake understood. He could have kissed the old man right on the spot.

Now, brother, he could look at the stars all he wanted to. And maybe, too, at Howie and the others.

**43**

He started to walk through the shadows to the front of the shop, when old man Gold called out after him, "Take care of the eye. It's all puffy."

He wanted to take a closer look at the shop on his way out. But he couldn't. Not after that.

After that, stopping and looking would have been sacrilegious. Like looking a gift horse in the mouth.

# Chapter 8

When he came home after that first day in the shop and creaked his way up the apartment stairs, hoping to sneak into the bathroom before she could spot him from the kitchen, her headquarters, and see the eye and the finger, Mama was there, wet towel knotted around her forehead and all, waiting, expecting the worse.

He did his best to hide the eye and, for a few seconds anyway, thought he'd succeeded. He struck up a truly magnificent, military pose when he saw her at the top of the stairs, his right arm cocked at the side the way he'd seen Marine officers with swagger sticks cock theirs, his heels planted firmly together at right angles on the fifth step. He saluted smartly and reported, "Mama, I got a job today. At Gold, Inc. I'm an embosser."

His head, of course, was turned to the stairway wall, so that the right side of his face was buried in shadow.

She seemed at first almost to smile, as though to say, "Well, isn't that nice. The last of my sons is a man now, working."

But the smile was deceiving. In fact, when he thought

about it more, Jake was certain there'd been a mistake. She hadn't smiled at all. She was sneering, that's what.

Because she didn't say it was nice. Nothing of the sort.

She barked was what she did. He'd never heard her bark like that before.

"God should help me," she barked. "I've been worried to death, with an air-raid practice tonight yet, and the streets black like the night because who knows when they'll bomb us, and you not home. A person can go crazy, not knowing. Are you trying to drive me crazy?"

It was a question Jake couldn't answer, not knowing whether he was or wasn't driving her crazy. Knowing only that he had a job and was getting forty-five cents an hour and couldn't hide his eye and his finger from her much longer.

He apologized so profusely, not wanting to hurt her, she broke into tears, which confused him, too, since forty-five cents an hour was nothing to sneeze at, especially when you remembered that Max had gotten only three dollars a week working at Weinberg's. And that was *before* the war.

But Mama, of course, didn't know that.

Maybe if Jake told her, the tears would cease and what he thought had been a smile would in the end turn out to be exactly that.

He sidled up the remaining stairs, having given up on the Marine Corps stance and keeping his bad side with all the wounds of his own little skirmishes out of sight, and let himself be clutched by her outstretched, quaking arms.

It felt good, being smothered like that.

Jake couldn't remember the last time she'd done it, unless it was on one of those mornings when Max or Michael or Benjy, each in his own way, had slithered, evaporated out of the house to become parts of the United States Army.

So, against her heaving bosom, before she'd seen either

**46**

the eye or the finger, he told her. "I'm embossing desk pads at Gold's, Mama, for forty-five cents an hour."

"Your Uncle Mordecai would turn over in his grave if he knew."

Jake's heart wasn't altogether in it, but he tried hard to mollify her. He knew what she meant about Uncle Mordecai.

He knew about Uncle Mordecai, Papa's brother with the earlocks and beard and broad-brimmed black hat, whom a rampaging Cossack had slain with a curved sword from atop a speeding white horse—only because Mama had told him so many times. Once the war had begun and she and Jake were home alone, on the days when he was sick and out of school, he would stay with her in the kitchen while she kneaded dough for a *challah,* a Friday-night braided egg-bread. She would speak almost to herself, about how it seemed there was always war; people didn't care about killing at all, they just did it out of some perversity of their natures that wasn't satisfied until they tasted blood.

Uncle Mordecai's wasn't a pleasant story—more blood-curdling, in fact, than most she told—because he had only been fourteen when the curved saber slashed through his innocent young neck. The Chief Rabbi of Warsaw—the Chief Rabbi, mind you!—came to Papa's house to mourn with the family, bidding them all to sit down in his presence, even though usually such a thing would have been sacrilegious. Uncle Mordecai, before his untimely death, had been one of the most promising young scholars, rabbinic students, the Chief Rabbi had ever met. And in the house where such a young man had lived and now was dead, people didn't need to stand in the presence of the Chief Rabbi. If anything, the Chief Rabbi should have stood in theirs—or, at least, in the presence of the young man's body.

So he knew what she meant by Uncle Mordecai. Jake was

already trying to figure out ways to persuade her that, if she'd only be patient, she'd see there was still some hope left for her last and only to live up to his uncle's image.

Then the little light coming into the blackened hallway from the kitchen must have hit Jake's face.

That's when she saw the eye. Not the split, blood-hardened fingernail yet. Only the eye.

Her tiny, pink mouth dropped open. The hands that had scrubbed so much laundry, piece by piece on a scrubboard in the bathtub, flew to her pale-from-the-daily-news-of-the-war cheeks, and there rose out of her such a shrill, piercing, chilling shriek, everyone in the whole neighborhood must have heard it.

"Oy vey!" she shrieked. "O-y v-e-y!"

A long, mournful cry that came from the abcess of all her past miseries, directed at the world as much as at Jake, rending the apartment like a bolt of lightning.

Jake practically shriveled up at the mournfulness of it, it made him feel so bad, so much like a criminal.

Oh, the next time, Howie. The next time. Things will be different the next time, Howie Woscowicz. Your mother will be the one who screams the next time. Wait.

Mama couldn't wait. Even as the echo of the shriek reverberated off the walls like dying thunder, her scrubboard fingers probed, stroked, rubbed, tested the pulpiness of the eye.

For her sake, Jake refused to wince, to grimace, even at the needles of pain that shot through the eye with each touch of her fingers.

He smiled instead.

"It's nothing, Mama," he said as, her hand gripping his elbow now, she led—no, pulled—him into the apartment, into the kitchen, for a more complete examination.

**48**

"How?" she said. "When? Where?"

The questions hit Jake like bullets: fast, dangerous. He hardly knew how to answer.

The big war—the *real* war—was enough. She didn't need one of her own now with Mrs. Woscowicz downstairs. Nor did she need to know—with all the worry she already had about the fate of her other sons and of her relatives still in Europe who, maybe, had already been killed by Hitler's hordes—about the urinating in Humboldt Park or even about the dare that had sent Chris up that telephone pole.

Those didn't need to be her kinds of crises.

As calmly as he could, Jake said only, "It's nothing," again. One more time and then, after a pause to steel himself against any other "oy veys," added, "I tripped in gym, playing baseball, and hit it on the fence."

It must have been just the right touch, precisely the right thing to say, exactly what was needed, because Mama then shook her head, dropped Jake's hands, *tsk-tsk*ed several times, sat him down at the table and, as though nothing had happened, said, "Eat!"

He did. And she looked at the eye now and again, *tsk*ed some more, and wondered what the world was coming to that he had to work in the "glue factory."

Jake listened and didn't interrupt to say anything on old man Gold's behalf. He was too hungry and tired.

# Chapter 9

They were, those first three or four weeks at the shop, like being in a different world.

It wasn't only the green light of the place—converging on and permeating everything, including the brown roaches that scurried around and under the gluing machines—that made the difference.

Or the peeling green plaster of the walls with, here and there, the scribbled initials or names and dates of all those who'd gone before.

It was . . . it was, well, the whole feel of the place: the tightness of it, the closeness; the hum of the machines, the smell of the glue, the constant chatter.

And the music.

Old Izzie Gold's opera records, especially when the leg bothered him, were part of it, too.

Always, in the background, was Harry Katz, of course.

In the beginning, though, there wasn't time for Harry Katz.

The shop, in the beginning, was everything.

The shop, in the beginning, was old Izzie Gold: bald-headed, limping, loud-voiced Izzie Gold. The commander in chief. The general, leading an army different from the ones the big, black headlines screamed about in the newspapers. Or that were talked about on the radio. Or shown—bloodied, fatigued, dying—at the Vision Theater whenever the Pathé news came on with its cock-a-doodle-do rooster.

But an army nonetheless.

And when Jake ran from Lafayette to the shop, it was like running across the infiltration course Benjy wrote home about, where pretend enemy soldiers fired pretend bullets at you to get you ready to face the Nazis or the Japanese.

Because always there was Howie to be avoided, and the other two members of the Francisco Avenue triumvirate, Gene and Stash.

The shop became Jake's training ground for the war with the dictators of Francisco Avenue.

And embossing was part of the training.

Jake thought about embossing and old Izzie Gold a lot.

He thought about them night and day.

At night, he woke up from dreams in a sweat, dodging blue-tongued flames from the embossing machine as though they were being spewed out by flamethrowers on a battle-field. He turned; he twisted; he plumped his pillow to find a dry, cool spot for his head.

In the morning, when Mama poked him to get up for school, he begged to sleep longer—"Oh, just another ten minutes, another fifteen minutes. Please?"

And at school, sitting through arithmetic or social studies, he dreamed, too, about the paratrooper boots that Michael wore in the photograph he'd sent home that stood so heroi-cally on the mantel above the fireplace, in the shadow of the three-starred flag, and swore to himself that as soon as he earned enough money from embossing, he'd buy himself— provided Mama had enough ration coupons for them—high-top boots just like Michael's. With a knife, too, in the pocket at the top of one boot.

Miss Robertson and Mrs. Devine and Mr. Swiatek grew impatient and kept having to remind him, "Jacob, pay attention to your work or I'll have to send for your mother."

Jake tried hard to pay attention, to get all the spelling words right and all the arithmetic problems, too, because if Mama came to school, apart from the embarrassment of her fractured English, there'd be no more shop. Pure and simple. There'd be only more crises. And he couldn't have stood that. Because after a month, frankly, the shop was in his blood.

So that, at the beginning of June, he raced into the shop one day as usual to punch in at exactly three-fifteen and found himself staring into the thick-jowled face of Izzie Gold, not believing what Izzie Gold was saying.

"You'll work here full time in the summer, Ackerman, do you hear? I need someone with good hands."

A record spun on the Victrola turntable, and old man Gold's voice rose and fell with the rhythm of the tenor singing. And Jake, seeing that some of the other guys whom he knew by name only as Aggie and Alex and Goose and Jedge were watching from the edges of their eyes, blushed.

God, he blushed!

The general was promoting the private, right in front of the rest of the troops, and the private couldn't stand all the sudden fame.

"Okay," he whispered. "Sure, Mr. Gold."

Already he was multiplying the forty-five cents an hour

times the eight hours a day times the five (maybe six?) days a week, and subtracting from it the money he'd give Mama. Those high-top boots with the pocket near the top for a knife . . . he could already feel them clinging to his legs, when and if he ever decided to strut down the street to face the enemy, to close in for an attack, getting set to blow the three of them to smithereens.

He'd get them yet. Just wait.

And at that minute, at that precise second in June 1943, all of it began to take shape. With old Izzie Gold slumped in the seat near the desk, with the good and the bad legs stretched out in front of him, and his hands in his lap and the music in the background, and the order to work full time in the summer still in the air, making the heads at the long, green table turn—in envy, maybe, or elation, it didn't make a difference which—so that Jake really, for the first time, felt like he counted.

All of it seemed to coalesce right then, the business with Harry Katz and the two Bar Mitzvahs and Chris and the stars in the window.

Because right after old Izzie Gold said that—"You'll work here full time. . . . I need someone with good hands"—and Jake, maybe too cockily, aimed himself towards the back and the embossing room, that voice—the very first voice he'd heard inside Gold, Inc., over a month before—that same voice brushed over Jake's left shoulder and said, "So you're going to work full time this summer, huh?"

The voice was that of Harry Katz—so even, so steady, so absolutely certain of itself that Jake latched on to it at once, saying, "Yeah," but thinking, God, wouldn't it be something if the two of us together took on Howie and those guys?

And then, not a fraction of a second later, before Harry

even had a chance to nod, to part his lips to utter another sound, Jake, desperate to cement the two of them, added, "My name's Jake. What's yours?"

A mere formality, really, since each had heard the other's name screamed God-knows-how-many-times in the last month. But it was a start.

"Mine's Katz," the other one said. "Harry."

# Chapter 10

That's how Harry Katz got into it.

It couldn't have taken more than a second.

But it was enough to isolate Harry, to set him apart from the others at the long green table who were still strangers, except for the names Jake had heard them call each other on his daily lonely journey to the rear.

"Watch those Cubbies win the pennant, Aggie."

"Shit, Goose! This here is Sox territory. Better watch what you're saying. Right, Jedge?"

"Yeah? Well, Alex says the Bears are the ones to watch, kiddo. That Sid Luckman is something, ain't he?"

Because when Jake looked up to acknowledge Harry's name, to signal to him with a slight tilt of the head and a sheepish grin that he'd known it all the time, that's when he saw it—the tag end of a black yarmulke, a skullcap, sticking out of Harry's back pocket.

Something clicked.

Doggone, Jake thought. He's Jewish, too.

He shivered, Jake did, remembering how they'd almost bumped into each other that first day and there'd been a flash that this was someone he might be knowing for a long time. Suddenly he remembered what made him sense that—the tag end of the yarmulke had been sticking out of Harry's back pocket then too.

It felt like a blood oath in the making.

One of the guys at the table—the short, taut one with the bushy hair and blue coveralls, whom they called Aggie— broke away from the rest with a yawn that sounded like a snore, and started up the gluing machine. He ran a wet rag back and forth along the length of the two brass rollers until they glistened.

The gluing machine *whirr*ed.

Old man Gold turned off the Victrola and yelled, "So? What's everyone standing around for? A miracle?"

Jake, halfway towards the embossing room, couldn't let it end, not now. Not without some sort of additional confirmation from Harry Katz. He had to say one more thing, he had to try one more strategy to keep the conversation going.

"You going to work full time this summer, too?" Already he envisioned the two of them confronting Howie Woscowicz together. A team. A commando party arming for a sneak attack on a rocky coast. God! What an idea!

"Don't know yet," Harry said. "I'm studying for my Bar Mitzvah. It depends."

At least it wasn't final. At least it wasn't over, never again to be started. There was, at least, still a chance.

So Jake took it, leaving the door wide open.

"Yeah," he said. "I might be studying for mine, too."

Like hell! He'd never even dreamed about it. But so what? Hadn't there been Uncle Mordecai? Wasn't that precedent

56

enough? Wouldn't it be worth it, just to be able to match the two of them up against the Francisco Avenue triumvirate?

Harry nibbled at it. No large, gulping bite that a person could choke on. Just a nibble.

"Great," he said.

Jake, ravenous, went after more. "Maybe . . . maybe," he said, "we can get together sometime, you know?"

Unmindful, oblivious almost to old Izzie's yell still echoing in the shop, this other need was so great.

"Maybe," Harry said. "Yeah, maybe."

That's all.

But it was enough. It was enough to send Jake—alive now to the steely-eyed stare of old Izzie on his back—scurrying to the embossing room, filled with a new feeling.

The flames back there danced in his face and cast ghoulish shadows on the walls lined with the rolls of Leatherette and lit up the frantic movements of the roaches.

Now, though, Jake didn't mind so much.

Now everything seemed more tolerable.

# Chapter 11

The war was raging on.

Like a link in a chain, it joined Jake to the shop and Harry Katz and the idea of a Bar Mitzvah.

All of them came together, in fact, that very night when, climbing the stairs to the apartment above Howie Woscowicz's, Jake heard the shriek—tiny, piercing, skin-tingling.

Mama, a cleaning rag still in her hand, the wet towel as always around her forehead, stood in the doorway facing Papa.

The shriek lay curled on her lips like a squiggling worm. She didn't hear, she didn't see Jake coming. Immobile, petrified, she stared at Papa, home for the dinner that separated his two defense jobs.

Papa, too, looked different. His floppy straw hat sat precariously on the crown of his head. One heavy, blue-veined hand stroked the furrows in his forehead. The other clutched a folded piece of paper. His jaw twitched.

The two of them, facing each other just inside the partly

opened door, looked, indeed, like wax figures in a museum: clammy and sallow.

The shriek froze Jake with one foot on the landing and the other on the step below. He was afraid to run up. He was afraid to run down.

Something is *really* wrong this time, he thought.

This was, from the sound of it, one of Mama's real crises. Bona fide and tested, equal, maybe, to the rampaging Cossacks in the Polish village of Viskov. Who knew? It might even be a greater one.

Her breath came fast and hard, like tiny bursts of air from a furiously pumped bellows.

"Why?" she cried. "God, why?"

Jake began—noiselessly on the carpeted stairway—to lower his uppermost foot, to withdraw, to flee the knot tightening in his throat.

Because . . . because an invocation like that, to God himself, had to mean trouble of the worst kind. Mama would not use it lightly.

One of them is dead! he thought. Max or Michael or Benjy is dead!

The thought was so horrifying, so numbing, so incredibly overwhelming, he had to grab for the bannister to keep from falling backwards down to the bottom of the stairs. He clung to it fiercely until his knuckles ached, until they hurt so much they felt as though they would break through the skin.

Which of the ones who had evaporated into the darkness of morning with a "So long, sport!" was dead? Which one wouldn't come back? Which emptiness would never be filled again?

Papa, seeing Jake, stirred. He took a step from the doorway. Not a long, bounding, powerful step. A dragging, nearly imperceptible one that brushed against the carpeted floor, made a sushing sound.

He thrust his one blue-veined hand towards Jake, the other dangling at his side with the folded piece of paper rustling against his trousers.

Jake stared into his eyes for a clue, a hint. He moved up to meet the outstretched hand.

Their fingertips met.

Jake couldn't remember the last time they'd done that or anything like that—touching.

Papa said, "Your brother Max has been wounded. He'll be all right, the telegram says. That's all."

It wasn't all, really.

Papa's cold fingertips said more.

But twelve-year-olds weren't supposed to know more. Twelve-year-olds were supposed to be seen, not heard.

That's what Papa had always said.

"Will Max come home, Papa?" Jake said. "Will he live?"

There were other questions he wanted to ask too, like, "Were his brains spattered, like Chris's? Will his name be in the paper on the casualty list? Did he win a medal?"

But Papa's lips were sealed; his jaw twitched; his eyelids sagged under whatever he was thinking.

So Jake turned to Mama. He wanted to give her back the hand she'd dropped that Saturday of Chris's fall from the telephone pole, the hand she'd made no effort to retrieve. knowing, as she must have, that things like that had to happen, that sons grew up and left.

He touched her arm—rippling above the elbow with fat— and looked at her.

Her eyes were pink and puffy.

She grabbed him and moaned "Why?" again and again.

And though he could feel the beat of her heart against him and the soft heaving of her body, he understood, with that understanding that creeps in like a chill, a fever, that she wasn't holding him at all. She was holding Max. Or Michael. Or maybe Benjy. Or all three of them—her soldier sons—together.

Jake clung hard to her, trying to squeeze the trembling from her.

She clung back.

But somehow it wasn't the same.

When she pulled away, he had no choice, no alternative, but to say the thing he said, knowing Papa's love for the records of Cantor Yossele Rosenblatt and for his dead brother Mordecai, and Mama's passion for the ritual of the Friday cleaning and, at least in the old days, preparations for the Saturday-evening meal.

"I'm going to go to Hebrew School with a friend at work, Harry Katz." He tossed the name off easily, to give it a truly familiar ring, and then waited for it to sink in. With any kind of luck, it might take their minds off the piece of paper Papa still clutched.

They didn't move. They didn't stir.

That's why Jake stammered on. "And . . . and," he said, "I'm going to study for my Bar Mitzvah. You'll be proud. You'll see."

It was an impetuous, risky thing to say.

But it was an impetuous, risky time.

Papa finally unsealed his lips. His eyes widened just so much. No more. No less.

"That's fine, Jacob," he said. But the blue-veined hand clutching the telegram still trembled, and the voice had a hollow ring to it. "Maybe," Papa said with the pretense of a chuckle, "maybe we'll have a rabbi in the family yet."

**61**

Jake, tight and clammy all over now just like the two of them, backed away from Mama.

"You'll see," he said. "I might be . . . if I try. If I want to."

Mama put her fingers into Jake's hair, massaged the curls that he would have given anything in the world to exchange for a good old-fashioned army crew cut like Harry Katz's, and said, "Papa, maybe . . . maybe our little Jacob takes after Mordecai—God rest his soul. Hannah Rachel will finally have someone to give her prayer shawl and prayer book to."

Papa waved the free hand, the one without the telegram in it. "It would be a nice thing," he said. "A good thing. But now we should eat so I don't get to the plant late."

Jake began to plot again. He dreamed about his Great-aunt Hannah Rachel's prayer shawl and prayer book being presented to him with the whole synagogue thunderously applauding.

The din of it made his head spin.

"I can do it," he kept repeating to himself. "I've got to do it."

# Chapter 12

He couldn't keep it all to himself.

Either Max's being wounded or the idea about the Bar
Mitzvah.

On the day he began working full time, he said to old Izzie
Gold: "My brother's been wounded. But we got a letter, and
he won the Purple Heart and he's okay. And I think I'll get
Bar Mitzvahed."

Old Izzie set a roll of Leatherette down and limped over to
Jake's stool. He stood there—it seemed like forever—staring
into space.

When he finally spoke, he was almost chanting: "People!
People, they love killing, don't you know?"

Jake shuddered.

He tried to but couldn't say any more. How could he?
How could he say there'd been times when he wanted to kill
Howie? And Gene? And Stash?

"So you let the music in—don't you see?—to make you
forget the killing." Izzie was practically whispering. "To
help you forget." He drew the words out so that they
sounded like a prayerful refrain. "And," he said, "you make

everything into something. Something you can look at and say, 'See, I made this.' If you can look back on things you made, it makes something like finding out your brother is wounded easier."

A long silence followed. Jake said, "Were you ever wounded in a war, Mr. Gold?"

Izzie Gold peered at the peeling plaster, his eyebrows arched in contemplation.

"Not wounded." He laughed. "Never wounded. In the old country, though," he said, "in the old country, when I was your age, I was an ice skater."

Jake squirmed on the stool, waiting.

Old Izzie, leaning up against a roll of Leatherette, ran his fingers over a stretch of it, examining it, smiling. "Then a boyfriend knocked me down with his sled—he didn't want me to be an ice skater as good as him—and the hip, the hip . . ." The words trailed off. He let the roll of Leatherette go and pointed to the bad leg. ". . . But I was never wounded in a war. No. Not in a war."

Jake wanted to tell him he was sorry, but somehow it didn't seem like enough. Somehow it was superficial, useless. So he said nothing.

Old Izzie, clutching the roll of Leatherette he'd been leaning on, turned to leave. "Everything into something," he murmured. "If you can't ice-skate, you do other things. It goes that way sometimes."

He limped to the door and paused.

"Bar Mitzvahs? Who knows? Me, I didn't have one. Maybe they make a man. Maybe not."

Jake started embossing again, his arm moving the lever up and down mechanically. Up and down. Up and down.

He was afraid, and he didn't know why.

He was so lost in thought, he didn't see Harry Katz come

into the room until Harry said, a second time, "Twelve o'clock, kiddo. You going to lunch?"

Jake, gladdened by the company, swung on his seat and said, "Yeah. Sure. You want to eat together?"

Harry threw his arms up as though to say, What kind of question is that? "That's what I came back here for, kiddo," he said.

Jake followed after him, cowed, shaky, but exuberant anyway to be going out to buy lunch for the first time in his life.

Now he was a full-time worker, not some rinky-dink baby who couldn't do anything on his own. The only question was: What about the sway of Harry's shoulders? Was that the way you did it when you were making forty-five cents an hour?

# Chapter 13

The steam rose up from the sidewalk and wrapped the two of them in a shimmering aura of light.

Harry's arms swung strong and easy at his sides. Shadows from the low buildings on the left covered half his face, leaving in bright sunshine the side nearest Jake, who couldn't look at it without wondering what a person had to do to get to look that way, so . . . well . . . so damned grown-up.

He thought maybe he should begin by tucking his chin in a little, like Harry. So he did. Then the shoulders. Harry's were pulled back, pushing the chest out and hollowing out the belly. Jake pulled his shoulders back, too. The problem was, his chest didn't puff out as much as Harry's. As for his belly . . . well, that didn't make a difference anyway. Some were hollow, some weren't, that's all.

The two of them blended into the life of the street.

People sat in chairs or on the thresholds of doorways all along the street, fanning themselves with newspapers or sucking on Popsicles or drinking lemonade from glasses that sweated glistening droplets. Some had mesh flyswatters edged in red or blue cloth in their laps, at the ready—oh, just waiting—for a blue-tailed fly to light within reach. Others fiddled the minutes away with their fingertips tapping against each other, their eyes following with a snicker every passing person. Some kids—who didn't have sense enough to act their age—raced deliciously through fire-hydrant geysers that pelted away their sweat.

A peddler lugged his half-empty cart on the east side of the street, between the kids in the water and the adults slumped in their chairs. "Rags for buying," he screamed hoarsely. "Umbrellas. Old clothes." He was a stubble-faced, hunch-backed man whose tattered pants were held up by frayed suspenders.

The yellow-and-green North Avenue Ice Company truck, with its small, square, gas-ration stamp in the center of the windshield, chugged down the middle of the street, right over the streetcar tracks. The driver's elbow rested on the ledge of the door window, his eyes barely open. Four guys following the truck with picks chipped away at the blocks of ice covered with straw in the rear of the truck. Every once in a while, they glanced around the side of the truck at the driver, to see if he knew they were there.

He was too sleepy to know.

Once the truck passed from view, Harry pulled up short and said, "Those idiots! They ought to arrest guys like that."

Jake, with his hands deep in his pockets, nodded. He guessed that if Harry said it, those guys must be doing something wrong, but he was hanged if he didn't envy them anyway, with that cold taste of the ice on their lips.

Still, he nodded. Harry, a whole head taller and seeming closer to fifteen than to thirteen, was as intimidating as old Izzie.

"They sure should," Jake said with much more enthusiasm than he felt. He wanted desperately to keep the conversation going.

Harry went on swaggering, if anything, even more. "What say we get a kosher hot dog over at Moishe's?" he said.

Jake felt it all now, all the rush of this new life coursing through him.

Jacob Ackerman going to Moishe's for hot dogs!

Damn!

The universe of Francisco Avenue, widened only weeks before to include Crystal Square and the shop, was on the verge of expanding even farther to Damen, near the Biltmore Theater. The thought of it—the Biltmore—dredged up memories of conversations between Max and Michael and Benjy about dates, about girls: "That Debbie can sure schnoogle if you get her in the back row of the Biltmore." "Aw, says you. Millie, now she's something else. She wears sweaters when we go there."

"Sure," Jake said. He drooled the word out.

He didn't dare ask if the quarter in his pocket was enough for a hot dog, at Moishe's Hot Dog Stand or any other stand for that matter. Not now. Not when he stood at the very brink of a new life.

No more Buck Rogers weekly serials for him.

He straightened up, the tucked-in chin and drawn-back shoulders feeling a little more comfortable, a little more natural.

It was a question of practice, that's all, of getting used to things. Then . . . why then they became natural and you didn't have to worry about getting there. You just did.

Harry stuck a hand in his pocket and jangled what sounded like a ton of coins.

They jangled marvelously, like the bells of Saint Fidelis chiming out a new time, the passage of time.

But how could you jangle a single quarter?

Jake was embarrassed.

His chin sagged. His shoulders dropped.

Harry was eyeing him.

So he yanked that single quarter out of his pocket and did the first thing, the only thing, he could think of. He set the quarter carefully between the knuckle of his thumb and the tip of his forefinger and tried—God, but it was difficult!—to flip it, propel it up into the air with élan and dash and dexterity, just that amount of skill he struggled to remember his brothers—he couldn't remember which one or ones—using.

The damned quarter spun crazily in the air before tailspinning to the sidewalk with a humbling *clang, clang, plop.*

Jake was glad to have to bend over and kneel down to pick it up. At least Harry couldn't see his face.

He waited for Harry to say the inevitable, to cry out "Klutz!" Or something even worse.

But Harry was already several steps ahead, swaggering on towards Division Street as if nothing had happened. As if the thing weren't even important enough to comment on.

Jake tagged behind. He whistled once or twice, trying to make light of his ineptness. But he couldn't even get the lousy whistle right. It sputtered from the edges of his lips: *P-s-s-t.*

When they got to where Arnie's Liquor Store was, with the sunflower-seed machine shackled to the wall, Harry said, "We better get going, kiddo."

Jake had to lean closer to him to catch all the words, because the Division Street trolley was making its screeching turnaround back east.

That's when, bent to the side with his hand cupped to his left ear to catch Harry's words, he saw, strutting down Division Street from Francisco, the gruesome threesome: Howie, Gene, and Stash, wearing their peg-legged trousers, their shoulders bobbing in unison like boats on a swell.

Jake gasped. He wanted to hide, to somehow secret himself in Harry's shadow so that the threesome would see only Harry and, not knowing him, go bobbing along on their merry way. He began to inch over and line himself up exactly behind Harry's body.

But Harry didn't understand what was going on. He gave Jake a quizzical look, his lips parted, his eyebrows arched.

Jake blushed. He couldn't go through with it. He couldn't, as much as he wanted to, hide in Harry's shadow.

He *ahem*ed, smiled, and said, in answer to the question on Harry's face, "I know those three guys coming here."

Harry craned his neck to see.

When he turned back to Jake, he looked different. The tucked-in chin sagged a little; the face was more flaccid.

"Hey," he whispered. "I know those guys, too. That one in front, the one with the pointy nose, he's always coming over to Von Humboldt School looking for fights."

After, Jake thought, after he's run out of sissy guys like me at Lafayette. He glanced quickly, shamefully, at his split fingernail.

The knot in his throat grew harder. He laughed. "Well, if they want to start something, we can handle them, right?"

He shook in his pants, but he said it anyway. They—he and Harry Katz—were a team now, weren't they? A commando group? It wasn't going to be like the school yard. Not now. Not here on the corner of Division and California. Not if they were smart. Not if they knew the junior commandos were working full time at Gold, Inc.

Howie and Gene and Stash came within shouting distance, their shoulders cocked, bobbing up and down. "Hey, Ackerman," Howie yelled. "That your new girl friend?"

It stung. Jesus, did it sting! Jake's knees buckled.

He waited; he hoped Harry would say something, anything, like "Let's kick the shit out of those bastards for saying stuff like that in public."

The threesome's pace quickened. The distance between them and Jake and Harry evaporated like the steam coming up out of the sidewalk.

Harry opened his mouth to speak.

Jake hung on for the words he prayed would come out.

"Let's beat it!" Harry said hoarsely. "Follow me."

Jake stood there, paralyzed. He couldn't believe it. Running away wasn't how you made everything into something, for pete's sake! That wasn't the way you fought wars, for Chrissakes!

But things were happening too fast to think.

Harry had begun to run. Had he begun to run! He was heading not towards Moishe's Hot Dog Stand or, for that matter, the shop, but north along California.

"Follow me!" he screeched over his shoulder.

Jake followed, sucked into the wake of Harry's voice.

He ran so hard, so fast, his heart pounded right up into the dried-out, searing lining of his mouth, all the way to his temples.

The gruesome threesome raced after them, in long, lean, angular strides that covered twice as much ground in half the time, along the green bushes that formed the boundary of Humboldt Park on the west side of California Avenue.

The two-story flats on the other side of the street streamed past in one long, steamy blur: brown, gray, red; wood, concrete, shingled.

Jake ran, pain hammering through each leg as it struck the pavement, converging on his groin in such excruciating tightness, if he could have, he would have doubled over right then and there and screamed.

But no one would let him.

Not Harry, who by now had such a head of steam up, he was nearly half a block in front of Jake.

Not Howie and the others, who, smirking even in the sweat of the race, closed in from behind like foxhounds.

Jake—gasping, choking for breath—ran and ran and ran, thinking only, Don't fall, for Chrissakes. Don't lean over too much. Don't let the legs give out or the vultures will be at you in a minute.

Adrenalin poured into his body, into every crevice of it, propelling him forward, farther and faster. Closer to Harry, nearer to wherever Harry was leading him. So close, in fact, he began to hear the rush—the puffing, huffing rush—of words streaming at him from over Harry's left shoulder: "Hebrew School . . . the *Shul* . . . It's . . . a . . . It's one . . . more block. On . . . the . . . right."

Harry's arm, beaded with shimmering sweat, pointed to a huge, gray building up ahead, opposite the park.

The leader led. Jake followed, a tiny, insignificant sliver of metal drawn to the poles of the magnet, whether it wanted to be or not.

Somehow or other, the two of them made it. They skittered across the tracks just in time to beat a clanging streetcar, whose conductor, his face twisted in anger, peered down at them. Temporarily, the car blocked Howie and the others' pursuit.

Harry and Jake made it across the street to the huge gray building on the corner with the two holy, concrete scrolls on either side of the massive mahogany doors and the inscription, etched in the marble lintel above the doors, GALICIAN CONGREGATION.

Harry had barely enough breath left to puff out, "Let's go in the back way, up the stairs. They'll never find us."

Some part of Jake—some distant, tiny part of him that wasn't numb from fatigue, that didn't stab with pain—knew it was all wrong. Drastically, shamefully wrong.

That long-ago wail from the top of the telephone pole flitted through his mind, then disappeared, because he and Harry were rushing through the back door of the synagogue and up two and three aching stairs at a time, a staircase so narrow, so strange, that Jake, when he reached the top of it, thought he'd suffocate up there.

But not Harry Katz. Harry Katz looked right at home. He stopped gasping. His chest stopped heaving. He broke into an imperious grin.

"Let them try and get us here," he said.

Jake wished he could believe him. Because if he was going to get killed retreating from the front line, it would be just as well that it happened in a narrow stairway where the world would never find out the truth of it.

But he didn't. He didn't believe Harry at all. He knew, just as surely as he knew he wanted to vomit, that the gruesome threesome would be there in a jiffy to wipe the two of them out.

And he would have said so, too, if it hadn't been for the accidental, chance turn of his neck, to relieve a cramp, that brought his eyes to focus on a thing in the classroom to their right: an orange, flickering light above the Holy Ark at the front of the room. He didn't know what the light was for.

"What's that, Harry?" he whispered.

"The Eternal Light," Harry said. His face lit up. "It burns forever over the Ark with the Torah in it. It is God's way of showing us we're His Chosen People."

Jake's mouth opened in awe. He stared at Harry. "No kidding, Harry?" he said. "You're not putting me on?"

Harry didn't get a chance to answer.

The door down below squeaked, creaked open, letting a sliver of sunlight into the darkened stairway. The shadow of an arm came next. Then Howie's whole body appeared.

A question was already on Jake's lips. "What do we do now, Harry?"

But he needn't have asked.

Harry already had the situation in hand.

He ripped the red fire extinguisher off the wall opposite the classroom, aimed the hose down the stairs and, with Howie and Gene and Stash smugly making their ascent, began pumping, pumping, pumping.

The foam, the powerful spray of it, spattered off their faces, off the walls.

It was beautiful.

It reminded Jake of the litter basket in the park with Howie's private spray shooting through the tiny hole in the wooden bottom.

The three of them stopped in their tracks. Stunned. Startled. Frozen. One of them—it was hard to tell which, their mouths were so full of the foam—yelled, "Let's get the hell out of this joint."

Trailing bubbles of baking soda behind them, they fled.

They fled so beautifully, so incredibly fast, Jake didn't know whether to cry or to laugh.

Maybe it didn't make a difference, having an advantage like that, being at the top of a hill firing down at the enemy, seeing them fall left and right. It happened like that all the time in war. Maybe it wasn't wrong at all. If they could do it to you, why couldn't you do it to them?

Harry put the fire extinguisher back up where it belonged.

"If Rabbi Shonfeld catches me, I'm done for," he said. "So let's go."

But Jake couldn't let it end like that, not without showing his respect.

"Thanks, Harry. Thanks a lot," he said.

Someone, finally, had vanquished the Francisco Avenue triumvirate.

Sneakily, maybe. Cheaply, maybe. But so what?

# Chapter 14

They might have gone for those hot dogs still except for the clock at the bottom of the stairs, where the narrow stairway opened up on the left to the sanctuary.

But the clock was there and Jake saw it.

And he stopped, just for an instant, to look at it—hanging white and round over the box full of black yarmulkes—the hands pointing to 12:20.

"God's Chosen People," the clock clicked. "God's Chosen People have vanquished the Francisco Avenue trio."

Jake's thoughts raced. He said to Harry, "It's too late to get hot dogs now, Harry. I'm going to go find out if I can sign up for Hebrew School. There's time for that."

His stomach growled and the vision of Moishe's, as he imagined it from the long-ago tales of his brothers, filled him with great temptation.

But something else stirred him too. It's not the same as being in the army, he thought, but it's something. It's better than nothing.

Harry didn't answer. He opened the door a crack—wide

enough for a sliver of sunlight to be blinding—and peeked out.

When he saw the coast was clear, he took off.

Leaving Jake standing alone in that doorway to decide whether or not he ought to go find someone to sign him up for Hebrew School.

Because he had to do *one* thing, at least—having run all those blocks from the shop until his heart felt like a time bomb—to prove that he could make it into something.

Otherwise, he might as well be dead, for all the good he was doing.

Standing under the clock through another *click* of the minute hand, he drew in a deep breath and made his way down the corridor off the stairway, towards the only noise—other than the *click*ing—in the whole place. A *rat-tat-tat*ing so furiously fast it could have been a .50-caliber machine gun. Past a bronze IN MEMORIAM plaque with teardrop-shaped lighted bulbs on it beside the names of people like *Nettie Schwartz, 1895–1932; Abraham Prokovny, 1930–1939; Millie Danoff, 1939–1943.*

The teardrop-shaped bulbs gave off the only light in the corridor. They were eerie.

Jake trembled past the plaque, one leg after another, towards the *rat-tat-tat*ing coming from the other end.

Maybe they won't let me, he thought. Maybe they'll say I'm too old to start now.

And what about old Izzie Gold, about whether being Bar Mitzvahed made a difference or not?

Jake shook off the doubt and inched his way ahead, up to still another plaque, this one in a sunlit lobby dominated by a stained-glass window with a blue-and-white Star of David on it.

**77**

This plaque, with its gold letters deeply etched in the white marble, really gripped Jake, drawing him so close, he couldn't resist reaching out to it with his hand and running his forefinger into the grooves of the letters, the way old Izzie sometimes ran his fingers over the embossed imprints on the leather strips.

The marble plaque said, across the top: In Honor of Our Sons Killed in the Defense of Our Country.

It hurt to look at it, the letters were so brilliant.

Jake, head hanging, turned away to find the source of the *rat-tat-tat*ing.

It came from a room past the lobby, marked above the door with a simple sign: Office.

He hitched up his pants; wiped the tops of his shoes on the bottoms of his trousers; straightened, as best he could, the waves of his hair; finally despaired of the effort; and then shuffled into the room.

A black-haired lady sat at a desk with her back to the door, typing. Her fingers flew over the typewriter keys. Every couple of seconds, she gripped a lever at the top of the typewriter and flipped the carriage hard to the right.

Jake stood behind her a long time, waiting, rehearsing. I'll tell her I've been in bed three years with rheumatic fever, he thought. But that sounded too melodramatic. Well, then, he thought, I'll say it's the war. The war's interfered. Except he didn't know what the war interfered with or how.

The typewriter kept on *rat-tat-tat*ing.

God, she'd make a great machine gunner, he thought, imagining each *rat* and each *tat* of the typewriter keys to be a blazing tracer bullet striking right at the heart of the enemy.

She swiveled on her chair to get a sheet of paper.

She saw him.

Jake looked at her.

No Mrs. Weinberg, she. Plump-cheeked and huge-bosomed, she wore no makeup. When her lips parted in a small O to speak, the cheeks dimpled in a warm smile.

"Yes sir," she said. "What can I do for you?"

Jake said, "I want to get a Bar Mitzvah."

It sounded dumb, like someone coming into Weinberg's asking for a can of black-market salmon. But there was no other way for it than to plain get it out, stupid or not.

She didn't laugh. She went on smiling a dimpled smile and said, "Where did you go to Hebrew School before?"

Jake wasn't ready for the question. He leaned against the desk, crossing one leg over the other to steady himself.

Maybe he ought to tell her about Uncle Mordecai and the Cossacks. Or . . . or . . . maybe he ought to tell her he knew Harry Katz, and didn't she know they worked together at Gold, Inc. And . . . and that all his brothers were in the armed forces of the United States? Wouldn't a Bar Mitzvah be just the right touch? Something to add to the stars in the window?

He didn't. He fingered some papers on her desk—not rudely, of course—and glanced around the office, at the file cabinets, at the bookcase with dried-up-looking books that resembled the *Gemara* Papa kept stored in the closet.

He even thought about bringing up Howie and the others. How could it hurt—her knowing how hard he was trying to defend the Chosen People against urination?

That, though, was a cheap shot, and he knew it. Being urinated on wasn't a hell of a lot worse than being fire-extinguished on when you didn't have any warning.

"I've never gone to Hebrew School, ma'am," he said. "But I can study hard when I have to. And my father's got a

*Gemara* at home and almost all the records of Cantor Yossele Rosenblatt, and I was just twelve a little while ago and I can do it in a year. I just know it.''

She laughed. Not meanly or viciously so that you felt like crawling, slinking away on your belly. But softly, rolling her head.

"Well, young man," she said. "I don't know. It's unusual, starting so late is."

"Yes, ma'am," Jake said.

"But I'll ask Rabbi Shonfeld when he comes in. In the meantime, you come back tomorrow and we'll see."

She winked at him and swiveled around on her chair, back to the typewriter again. "You look like a nice boy," she said over her shoulder. "With so many men being killed, God knows the rabbi will be happy."

Jake backed out of the office, silently praying. I hope to God he will be. I hope he will be.

# Chapter 15

Well, he was.

Rabbi Shonfeld, goateed and in a pin-striped suit, *tsk*ed a couple of times like Mama, when Jake came back the next evening; preached a brief sermon on the shamefulness of a twelve-year-old's having gone through all those years of his life without Hebrew School; and then, at the end, said, "Anyway, it's God's will, and for that I'm happy."

And Jake—remembering only vaguely now Chris Petropolous's wail because his own head was filling up with the sounds of Hebrew letters and vowels, to say nothing of the whole new way of reading from right to left instead of from left to right—Jake, that summer, became so busy, he had barely any time for thinking. If you subtracted the war, and Papa's almost always being away from the apartment on either one or the other of his two defense jobs, and Mama's constant concern over the real crisis in her life, namely that, at any time, any or all of her other sons might turn from being blue stars in the window into gold ones—if you subtracted all that, and in addition, Howie and Gene and Stash (temporarily, at least, fire-extinguished out of action), why, there just wasn't time to worry.

Old Izzie did his part, too, to fill up Jake's time by practically pulling him out of the embossing room one day and saying, "You start working up in front now. Making corners."

No smile. No schmaltzy talk, like "Ackerman, you're promoted." A tug at the shoulder, that's all, plus the *thump-swish* of the bad and good legs alternately meeting the floor, paving the way past the peeling plaster to the table where everybody else—Harry and Aggie and Goose and Alex and Jedge—worked. And then a mere jerk of the head toward Alex, to signal him that he was to replace Jake at the embossing machine.

Until, before he realized what was happening, Jake was ensconced at the end of the table farthest away from the gluing machine and the green window, with old Izzie hunched over him, holding him—clutching him almost—and guiding his hands, showing him how to pleat the strips of leather he'd only just learned to emboss, so that the leather would fit tightly and neatly around the rounded corners of the cardboard, which was already on its way to becoming a finished desk pad.

What if all the other guys—including Harry—were digging into him with their eyes like bayonets twisting deep into a belly, practically screaming, "How come, kiddo? How come, Ackerman, he treats you so special, bringing you up here with the rest of us when you've only been working here—what?—a month? Two?

Jake was damned if he knew why. He was too shocked and too busy to think a lot about it. Well, except for the rumor, the whisper he'd heard about old Izzie's own son—a real highflyer who couldn't stand working in his old man's glue factory; a 4F to boot, ineligible for the army because of fallen arches, who'd taken off for parts unknown, leaving old man Gold a vacuum that needed to be filled.

It didn't matter—much.

What did matter was that Jake was finally up there, out of the back-room inferno, and it felt awfully good. Just the idea of it, of being promoted, of its simply happening.

He could have basked in it all day long. Or maybe, even, for the whole summer.

But Harry, with his sly, surreptitious, furtive stares from the other end of the table, wouldn't let him.

It didn't make sense, the staring didn't, not after the blood oath that was signed with the yarmulke and sealed, first with the battle of the fire extinguisher and, only minutes later, with Jake's actually going in on his own to sign up for Hebrew School.

In fact, it hurt. That's what it did.

The others—Aggie and Jedge and Alex and Goose—didn't matter.

Jake had nothing to do with their Cubbies or Sox or pennant races.

But that black yarmulke hanging out, like a secret code word, from Harry's back pocket—Harry should have, must have, known what it meant.

He kept on staring anyway and it made Jake squirm. It made him want to stop everything—*CRUNCH,* like that—and go over to him and say, "Christ, Harry! Why are you so mad? What did I do? Old Izzie dragged me up here. I didn't do it on my own. And I don't know why he did it, either, so if you want to be mad, be mad at him."

He couldn't stop everything, though, because old Izzie hovered over him, clinging to him still, shoved a white bone folder into his hand and, meticulously, cautiously, taught him to use it to pleat leather corners as though they were sutures on a deep wound, sutures that, unless they were done right—just right, absolutely right—why, the patient would die.

So Jake had to concentrate on that, not Harry. He had to dredge up every last bit of attention left in him just to be able to let his hand and his fingers be guided by the gnarled hand coming out of nowhere over his right shoulder.

The fingers—spatulate and jagged-edged—were what Jake focused on, moving, despite their size, their misshapen form, as deftly as Mama's slicing through noodle dough.

"No, no, no! A folder is not a hammer, for God's sake! A machine gun! Hold it like a pen, see? Soft. Gentle. Like you're writing a letter."

Jake tried hard. But all those eyes taunted him. One klutzy move, one fumble, and they were set to pounce on him with a "He can't do it. Old Izzie's pet Ackerman can't do it. Hah, hah, hah!"

Like vultures, the eyes waited.

"And use the left hand," old Izzie said, "use this finger of the left hand to hold the leather still, see, so when you pleat the corner with the folder, the folder pushes the leather against the finger."

Like that. Just so.

Jake did it, by God, with that keg-shaped body of old Izzie's thrust tight against his back, a prod, a support that wouldn't let him go until he made everything into something. Slowly the stiff leather pleats took on shape, rising up from the rounded corner of the cardboard, evenly spaced, until there were six of them: each the same thickness, each the same height.

Old Izzie saw that it was good. "Now," he said, the music in his voice rising to the ceiling, "now we . . ." Not you. Not me. But we. ". . . Now we pound the pleats flat with the hammer, see, so the felt backing goes on smooth and even.''

Jake licked his lips. The tiny hammer, blunt-headed on both ends like a shoemaker's, was in his hand before he had time to know it was coming, sticking to his hand because of the glue still there from the folder. An extension, nearly, of the hand itself. Not a thing apart, a separate entity, but as much a part of him as his very own fingers.

And the hand over his shoulder that came from nowhere gripped his, hammer and all, and guided it with a *thump* in an arcing path through the air to the raised pleats.

The *thump* flattened the pleats and, voilà, a desk pad was born.

"The secret," old Izzie whispered, "the secret is to make the back of the pad look like it just happened, like nobody's hands touched it. . . ." The sound of his voice faded. "Like a recitative. Accidental. A work of art.''

The Victrola wasn't playing now. There were no records on it.

But the front of the shop was filled with music anyway. Jake heard it with each movement of his fingers, squeezing the leather up into one pleat, then another, and another still. Rubbing the glue that oozed out from between each pleat onto his fingers, then rubbing the glue from his fingers onto the green apron before clasping the hammer and *thump*ing the pleats flat.

Old Izzie touched Jake's shoulder—a mere brush of his heavy fingers across Jake's shoulder blade—and limped away. Again without a word, without another sound, of either encouragement or discouragement. Leaving behind him only a feeling—nameless, labelless—that swelled up inside Jake: things were right, things were good. Things were as they should be.

**85**

Except for Harry, on the other side of the table, squinting up from the work he should have been doing but wasn't because he was too busy etching lines of contempt into the chiseled-out features of his face.

Jake felt the scorn without knowing what it was. It sent chills through him, right in the middle of the good feeling, and he couldn't do a thing about it. Not without making a big hullabaloo about it in front of everyone else. And for what? For no reason at all, except that Harry maybe had gotten up on the wrong side of the bed and was taking it out on him.

So he kept at the pleating, hoping the lines of contempt on Harry's face would disappear, losing track of the others at the table and even of old Izzie, literally glued to his new job, trying to do it right.

The place had become so quiet, but for the *whirr*ing of the gluing machine and the occasional *thump* of a hammer on a pleated corner, it might have been a grave.

Then old Izzie limped back to the table. Not towards Jake. Not towards Aggie or Jedge or Goose, but straight towards Harry, like a gull honing in on a little fish just below the surface of the water, invisible to everyone else.

He let out an ear-piercing shriek. So loud, so great, so voluminous, it exploded off the walls and the huge front window.

"Botcher! Potcher! What the hell kind of work is this, Katz?"

Harry's face turned beet red.

Old Izzie practically ripped the desk pad Harry was working on right out from under Harry's hands and tore open each of the four corners Harry had pleated.

Jake was too frightened to look up.

"Six months you work here and all you do is botch, slop

up the job, like it's some kind of game. In six months, a person should grow up. Learn.''

All the heads around the table hung low, but none as low as Harry's. The statue had crumbled.

Jake's heart sank. Why is he being so tough on him? he thought. Why doesn't he leave him alone, for Chrissakes?

Old Izzie threw the desk pad down right under Harry's nose so that it landed with a *thwack,* shivered, then died.

"Do it over again, Katz. Do you hear? Pay attention to what you're doing. Get your mind off the Bar Mitzvah with the presents, and pay attention to the work. Or . . . or . . .''

He didn't finish. He stormed away from the table—*thump,* shuffle; *thump,* shuffle—and fell into the chair by the desk. He clutched his leg, as if trying to squeeze the pain out.

Not even the music would have helped now, either old Izzie or Harry, who slouched there on the stool by the table hiding his beet red face.

Jake pleated the corners as furiously as his fingers, still stiff and clumsy from the newness of the task, would let him, trying to obliterate the scene, hoping it would evaporate so he wouldn't have to think about which one of the two of them— either old Izzie or Harry—he ought to be worrying about more.

Then he felt the eyes on him again. The only ones that counted now: Harry's. And he raised his head from the desk pad so that old Izzie wouldn't catch him and returned Harry's stare. To comfort him, really. To tell him with a simple look, "Hey, Harry, I know what it feels like. I was smashed down in the gravel like that with Howie Woscowicz over me.''

That's all he wanted the look to say.

But it was dumb. Because that's not what Harry's staring

back said. His eyes weren't saying that at all. The guy was glowering still. Beet red face and all, he was glowering at Jake.

Jake tried to escape it, bending to his work again. But it wouldn't go away, the look in those eyes.

And then it came to him.

Jesus Christ! He's jealous. Harry's jealous of *me*!

It didn't seem possible. It was crazy even, Harry's being jealous of him. Of Jacob Ackerman, who would have given anything to be able to look like, to walk like, the guy.

Damn!

Jake wanted to get up and go over and tell him, "Howie and those guys would have shellacked me if it hadn't been for you, Harry. They would have."

But old Izzie was sitting there.

It was mostly true. They might have. If, that is, he and Harry hadn't run away to the Galician Congregation's synagogue to hide there behind a fire extinguisher. At the top of the stairs yet.

So why should Harry be jealous?

Jake stewed over it all day, not saying anything more to Harry, Harry not saying anything more to him.

But it had to come to something sooner or later.

And when old Izzie, at the end of the day, just when everybody was punching out, said to Jake, "Tomorrow, Ackerman, I put on Caruso's *Tosca* and show you a voice," Jake knew it was going to be sooner.

# Chapter 16

The sky was already darkening in the west with huge black thunderheads, when he and Harry headed from the shop towards Hebrew School. Lightning, in mighty, arcing trajectories, cleaved the sky in the distance.

A gray, ominous pall fell over the whole street as far down as the eye could see: eerie, frightening, full of the smell of rain. People scurried for cover.

Jake and Harry picked up the scent of the storm and quickened their steps, neither one able yet to talk to the other, too caught up in escaping the imminent storm to break the silence.

The thunder rumbled, tumbled, crackled. Lightning ignited the heavens, filled it with tracer-bullet tails that crisscrossed each other like fireworks.

They looked skyward, fascinated and frightened, in a jerk of heads. They *click-clack*ed rapidly down the sidewalk towards the Galician Congregation's synagogue and the Bar Mitzvah class.

Except for the two of them, the street was virtually empty.

Except for an occasional sidelong glance, each of them might as well have walked alone.

The distance between them crackled as much with what they needed to say to each other as it did with the electricity in the air. But they didn't get to say it. Not then.

They couldn't.

Because while they were speeding along like that, with their eyes turned to the sky, lightning struck. A blue white explosion ripped open the skies above them with a roar, a clap, a furor of noise. It was so loud, so thunderously great a riving of the sky, they froze on the empty street below it. Stopped cold, their arms and legs poised for one more step, caught like that in mid-movement.

An ear-ringing, kaleidoscopic stillness followed. With one will, one purpose, the two of them broke into a wild, frantic gallop, Harry leading, all the way to the synagogue, the rain driving into him and into Jake like a fusillade of bullets.

When they got there—soaked, sagging from the weight of the rain—Jake had all he could do to stand up straight, let alone break the icy silence between them.

It took Harry to do that. Once they got inside and shook the water from their bodies and reached over to the box near the clock and pulled out yarmulkes, it took Harry to say, "Goddamn Gold! What's he want anyway?"

He pampered his yarmulke into place on the crown of his head and screwed up his face until the square chin trembled. "I'm not going to take that crap from him." He looked right through Jake. "He can't do that kind of crap." He stood over the box of yarmulkes for a long time, staring into space, trying to catch his breath. "Wait'll I get Bar Mitzvahed. I'll leave that dump so fast, the old geezer won't know what hit him."

They were the most words he'd said to Jake all at once;

they poured out of him like the blood should have in the oath they hadn't even sworn aloud to each other yet.

Jake looked up at the clock. There was still time before class.

He took a handful of soggy sunflower seeds from his pocket and held them out to Harry.

A peace offering.

A conciliatory gesture.

Harry picked at two, at three, and began to crack them open.

Jake sucked his, perking up with the sting of the salt on his lips.

"What did you get so mad at me for?" he said.

He shivered from the driving rain, from the dankness of the clothes clinging to his body.

Harry's chin stopped quivering. He cocked his head towards Jake. "Me?" he said. "Mad? Who said? What are you talking about?"

Jake shrugged his shoulders. He didn't know. He searched for ways to say it, but they weren't there. The stars in the window were there. Mama cutting noodles was there. Papa always being away on the two jobs, that was there. But there was no answer to Harry's question there.

"I don't know," he said, remembering only the sidelong glances all day long, remembering only how good it felt getting promoted to the front of the shop, how shitty it felt knowing that Harry resented it. Jake crunched down hard on a sunflower seed. He put it to Harry the only way he could. "If you don't like the old man, how come you're working there?"

Harry laughed a stiff, lingering laugh. "Same reason as you, kiddo." He spit out the shell of another sunflower seed. "To make a little loot."

Jake nodded, wanting somehow to show that he knew what that meant, whether he did or he didn't. Sure, he wanted to make loot. It sounded right. It didn't have much to do with the cigar box and Chris up at the top of the pole and a few other things, but it sounded right.

He nodded. "Don't you even like it, though?" he said, compelled to maybe squeeze a little more into it besides the loot. "I mean, making loot is all right, but don't you even like it?" He came down heavy on *loot* so it would sound professional, as though he'd been using it all his life.

Harry's nostrils flared. He pulled his shoulders back hard and sucked in his belly so that his chest puffed out. "You kidding me, Ackerman? Listening to that old man screaming all the time? Do this. Do that. Like a general. Shit!"

Jake wrenched a grin up onto his lips.

"Yeah," he said. "I know what you mean."

Like hell he did. But it was nice anyway, just to pretend there, for a second, that they were in a foxhole, maybe in Sicily or somewhere, standing up to their knees in water the way the papers said GI's did, griping about the brass. Jake—awed and terrified—looked up to Harry, the experienced sergeant, for strength and courage. He, Jacob Ackerman, was the new replacement. Green. Raw. A recruit off the troop ship which had zigzagged across the Atlantic without getting torpedoed.

What did he know about strength and courage?

"If my dad hadn't made me, you better believe I wouldn't be working at Gold's."

Jake's admiration soared.

"Why did he make you, Harry? Why is your dad making you work there, anyway?" He leaned against the wall, no longer even thinking about the clock, his thoughts far off in that watery foxhole.

This was the way it happened, damn it! He remembered the V-letters from Max and Michael and Benjy that talked about how a guy could make friends with other guys he hardly knew, all because they got together in a barracks or on the battlefield and in a couple of hours or in a day or a week found out things about each other it could have taken years to find out otherwise.

The buddy system, they called it.

Jake tried it out.

"Why did your dad make you work there anyway . . . buddy?" he said.

Harry's face sagged, but no more than an experienced sergeant's would. "Him and Gold," he said, "they know each other from the old country. They used to ice-skate together all the time. So my dad says, after my mom runs off to marry someone else, my dad says, 'You work for him. Learn a trade. It'll keep your mind off stuff.' "

He squinted, then turned away from Jake to stare vacantly at the clock above the yarmulke box.

Jake started to say he was sorry, he didn't know Harry didn't have a mother at home anymore. The words were formed; they were on his lips actually. But he didn't say them. He couldn't bring himself to say them.

How were you supposed to tell your sergeant you didn't want to hurt him anymore? He was hurting enough already.

"Old Izzie's leg got hurt ice-skating," he said instead. "His hip or something got hurt."

He felt pretty proud changing the subject that way, away from Harry's mother. Until the thing hit him. Harry's father must have been the one who knocked . . .

He couldn't believe it. The thing was bizarre.

He shut it out of his head. He started toward the stairs.

Harry grabbed him.

"Hey, Ackerman," he said, "don't tell any of the guys there, huh?"

Jake thought he meant about his father's knocking old Izzie down when they were little kids.

"And don't tell old man Gold either, okay? He don't need to pity me about my mother, see?"

Now Jake was confused. "Sure, buddy," he said. He didn't have the foggiest notion what he was agreeing to. But he was glad anyway.

Because now, for sure, they were in the fight together. Maybe not fighting the same enemy, but in the fight together.

# Chapter 17

The only ritual at the shop was making everything into something, and the only sin was botching up the job. At Hebrew
School the rituals and the sins were too many to remember.

There was a ritual for this and a ritual for that. Blessing the
wine was a ritual. Washing your hands in the morning and
before eating was a ritual. Blessing bread and meat and vege-
tables, they were rituals. Praising God before putting on the
prayer shawl and after taking it off were rituals. Swaying
back and forth during prayer was a ritual, just as standing for
some prayers and sitting for others were rituals.

Jake was bombarded by rituals.

He couldn't keep track of them all.

And everything he couldn't keep track of became a sin.

He was a perfect pagan.

When he followed Harry upstairs after Harry's confession
about his mother, he was happy to finally have a real buddy.

Because Rabbi Shonfeld, standing in front of the room by
the Holy Ark under the Eternal Light with, as usual, a ruler
in his hand, didn't like pagans.

Jewish or not.

But the rabbi liked Harry, so much so that he called him Katzele when he entered the room with Jake behind.

"Katzele," he said, "I'm sure there's a reason for your being late tonight?"

"I was home with my father, Rabbi," Harry lied.

And Rabbi Shonfeld winked at him, as though he understood about fathers whose sons had been abandoned by mothers, and patted him on the yarmulke.

The Rabbi didn't pat Jake on the head or wink at him.

"It's a sin!" he said to Jake. "A boy starts to become a Jew so late, you'd think he'd want to live in the synagogue. What does this one do instead? This one tramps in here whenever he wants."

He waved his ruler menacingly.

Jake's face burned. There were all those others staring at him for one thing. But that wasn't it exactly, the thing that made him want to die. What made him want to die, right on the spot, was the treason: Harry's lying.

Harry sat down behind his customary desk at the front of the room, where he could really wave his hand to answer the rabbi's questions.

Jake started to slink along the wall to the back.

But he didn't get there; he didn't reach his seat by the back window.

The rabbi hooked him with another barb.

"Late bloomer," Rabbi Shonfeld called out. "Mr. Late Bloomer, did you memorize the words I told you to memorize, eh? You want to become a Jew so bad, a man so bad, did you memorize the words a Jew must know to be ready for his Bar Mitzvah, eh? Tell me that."

Jake shriveled up in the cold dankness of his clothes.

He knew the words, damn it! He knew them as well as Harry. Under the flashlighted tepee of his bedcover, he'd embossed *Bet Hamidrash* and *Ner Tamid* and *Aron Hakodesh* and *Minha* and *Maariv* and all the *berakhot* deep in his memory.

They jangled about in his head like a pocketful of coins.

*Bet Hamidrash* = House of Study; *Ner Tamid* = Eternal Light; *Aron Hakodesh* = Holy Ark; *Minha* = Afternoon Prayer; *Maariv* = Evening Prayer.

But he was too shriveled up; he couldn't put them into words. He stuttered. He stammered. He rocked from one leg to the other. He stared at the dark, varnished floor. The rabbi had him by the throat and he wriggled like a worm.

"Uh . . . uh . . . er . . ."

Titters and snickers rose up from the rest of the class.

The rabbi, victorious, brushed Jake aside with a final sweep of the ruler.

"A sin," he muttered. He stood near Harry's desk now, leaning on it, looking like God Himself.

Jake fell into his seat. Behind everybody, where no one could see him, he buried his face in a book and steeled himself for an hour of misery and torment.

The rabbi said, "Katzele, tutor him! Teach him what he should know; he wants to become a Bar Mitzvah *bucher*—a scholar—so much."

*Him!* Not Jacob Ackerman, but *him!* Jake cringed. Why? Why did Papa have to have a brother Mordecai? Why did there have to be a Great-aunt Hannah Rachel who was just dying to have someone in the family to give a prayer shawl to and a silver-covered prayer book?

Harry turned enough to the right so that Jake could see the smile on his face. "Yes, Rabbi," Harry said. "Okay, Rabbi Shonfeld," he said.

An angel like the ones in cemeteries.

The telephone in the rabbi's office rang, and the rabbi went to answer it.

Jake was exhausted. He went limp. When the rabbi passed him, holding that ruler, and disappeared into the office, all the words and phrases came back to him. But the mere proximity of the rabbi filled him with consternation and uncertainty.

Once more, he felt abandoned and alone. He wanted to assert himself, to bring himself once more into someone's good graces.

The rabbi came out of the office heavy-footed and announced, "I must go for a few minutes, class. Katzele is in charge in my absence, do you hear?"

He ran from the room, clunking down the stairway and banging out the rear door; and Harry, gloriously elated, took his place in front of the Holy Ark.

The minute that door banged shut, all hell broke loose.

Spitballs flew all over the place, arcing and fluttering through the air, thudding and popping wherever they lit.

Harry, who couldn't stand guys chipping away at ice on the North Avenue Ice Company truck, stroked his adamantine chin, then wadded up a spitball, sized things up, picked out a target, wound up and threw.

The spitball landed God-only-knew-where. There were too many spitballs—like antiaircraft fire—to keep track of.

Jake wanted to wad up one of his own, to hurl it with all his might, to join in the screaming, the frantic, contagious battle cries.

He tapped on the desk; his eyes darted about the room; he tried following the flights of the missiles.

Sergeant Katz had left him standing in that watery foxhole all alone.

"Hey, someone hit Katzele."

"Someone put a tack on the rabbi's chair."

"Katzele, teach the new kid a thing or two, like Rabbi said."

What an uproar! What an outburst there was of guffaws and jollity.

Jake couldn't take it. He eyed Harry hard. But Harry, wadding up another piece of paper, was too busy to notice.

Jake retreated to the back window overlooking the wet, glistening sidewalk outside, where Rabbi Shonfeld was bound to appear as soon as he was done doing whatever he'd gone out to do and where Jake could be the first to spot him and warn the others.

He leaned his nose into the window to cut out the reflections from the lights.

At least, he thought, I can warn them when the rabbi comes back. Being a guard was better than being 4F like old Izzie's son.

He cupped his hands tightly around his eyes and peered out the window intently, searching the glistening darkness for the first signs of the rabbi.

A shadow moved outside. It looked like . . . it could be . . .

Jake was certain! It was. It had to be the rabbi walking down there, coming back. He didn't notice the melee behind him anymore: not the chattering and clattering, not the screaming or the spitball throwing.

All he knew was what a good guard ought to do, how a guard ought to protect the rest of the camp from surprise raids. And . . . afterwards, maybe, win a medal for it.

So he yelled. He yelled so loud that the echo of what he yelled bounced off the walls of the room that had turned, without his even realizing it, into a morgue, and came crashing back down on him: "All quiet on the western front!"

That's what he yelled. Thinking it was cute, thinking it would show all of them—and Harry, too—he was one of them.

The echo faded.

The silence hit him.

He turned.

Rabbi Shonfeld was in the room already, the ruler, like a saber, raised diagonally across his belly.

Rabbi Shonfeld had heard him.

Jake had yelled and no one, not a soul, had warned him there was no need to. Harry was already in his seat, facing the rabbi, as if the melee, the bombardment of spitballs, hadn't happened at all.

Jake took one, two steps towards his seat. The whole thing was a dream, that's what it was. But the floor squeaked. Floors didn't squeak in nightmares.

The rabbi took one, two steps. *Squeak, squeak.*

They were in a race, the two of them were, to reach Jake's seat.

Rabbi Shonfeld won, with a thwack—a stinging, burning thwack across the forearm that sent strings of pain up Jake's arm.

Jake stumbled into his seat, too ashamed to scream out.

He kept the scream tight inside him until it wanted to burst out.

He kept it closed up inside. He knew old Izzie would have approved.

And then the rabbi screamed, "What kind of kids' game is this in the *Bet Hamidrash*? When I step out for a minute? Who started it?" And no one, not another soul in the room, said a word. Jake didn't either.

He wanted to.

But he didn't.

Who would have? What kind of soldier would have ratted on his buddy? Especially a buddy who was going to have to tutor him, to get him ready to become one of the Chosen People.

# Chapter 18

Old Izzie knew something was wrong.

When Jake punched in the next morning at seven-thirty and put on his apron and took his stool by the table along the wall, washing off the dried-out layers of glue from his white bone folder, old Izzie, who'd been up long enough already to have heated all the glue in all the glue pots, sat hunched over the morning paper, chewing on the butt end of a cigar.

His wire-framed reading glasses slid halfway down his nose. He pushed them back up. He wet the tip of his forefinger, then flipped the pages of the paper.

He said nothing at first.

Jake went on rubbing the white bone folder clean of caked-up glue until it glistened in the overhead light.

None of the other guys were there yet, and the shop was still except for the rustling of the newspaper as old Izzie flipped the pages and moaned through his cigar about this battle or that killing.

The thwack lay heavy on Jake's forearm like a nagging pus-filled wound ready to burst open.

Old Izzie didn't look up from the paper; he filled the passing seconds with puffed-out ringlets of smoke. Finally he said, "So, Ackerman. Something's wrong, eh? The cat's got your tongue again, eh?"

Jake hid his arm.

"Heck, Mr. Gold," he said. "It's only seven-thirty. I'm still sleeping."

Old Izzie smiled and licked his thick lips. He clucked his tongue, then shook his head as though to say, I know better, young man. You don't look sleepy to me. That's not the way a sleepy person looks, with his eyes wide open like he's seen a ghost and his shoulders pulled back like that, holding his breath. "What's the matter?" old Izzie said. "You got trouble at home again? Another brother wounded maybe?"

Jake leaned closer to old Izzie, drawn in by the voice that rose hardly above a whisper.

"No sir," he said. "My brothers are fine. Really."

"So?" old Izzie asked. "What then? What's the long face for then?" He flicked a ring of ash from the end of the cigar and went on turning the pages of the paper.

The voice was soft and delicate, like the threads of a spider's web. Jake was trapped in it.

"The rabbi whacked me with a ruler." He laughed. Not a rolling, thunderous laugh that explodes from the belly and makes the whole body quake, but a trickling one, dripping off the lips like water from a faucet. "And I . . . and I didn't do anything wrong."

The lie made him uneasy. He thought that maybe he should back up—just a little—and tell the whole truth, about how he'd been on guard duty and let the troops down.

Old Izzie didn't give him a chance. "That's something to be long-faced about?" he said. He began tapping on the table. "Worse things happen. . . ." He paused and turned towards the sun beaming through the green window. "The world's full of *tsuris*—troubles. A person can't run away from it all.''

Oh no?

Who said?

How come, then, Jake had run home and thrown up when the only thing left to see of Chris was his brains? How come he'd run away from Howie and Gene and Stash and hidden behind a fire extinguisher in Hebrew School? How come he didn't call Harry a liar, in front of everybody, so Harry would have gotten the thwack?

How come?

He rubbed his folder furiously. If wishing would make it so, he'd wish to hell that he'd learn not to run.

Old Izzie glanced at the time clock, then got up. It was seven forty-five, so he limped over to the desk and the Victrola to put on *Tosca*. He set the needle on the record and waited for the music—soft, willowy, tremulous like gossamer—to settle over the whole shop. He didn't look at Jake even now, but stared instead at the time clock, measuring, it seemed, something more than the passage of time, something more than the number of orders to be filled or deadlines to be met. From the tremor of pain rending his body, he might have been measuring the things a person suffered and survived and grew stronger by.

''Well, Mr. Ackerman,'' he said, ''if you want to quit Hebrew School, so go ahead. No one's to stop you.''

He said it with little conviction, as an afterthought almost. The music seemed to have captured his full attention.

Jake's folder slipped from his fingers.

Old Izzie had read his mind.

''Now me,'' old Izzie went on, ''I don't believe in all that stuff anyway. To me, it's empty, rituals like that, like Bar Mitzvahs. What's it mean? A kid gets up there in front of people and says a few words—'Today, I am a fountain pen'—and suddenly, by magic, he becomes a man? Pshew! To be a man, Ackerman, it's more than that. To be a man means to take responsibility, you understand me? Not to run away—from anything. To do a job—making desk pads, for instance—like your life depended on it.'' He coughed up mucus and spit it out into a handkerchief, then began puffing on the stub of cigar in the corner of his mouth. ''No botching, see? No coming in here, like some people, just to make the money, but to work, to make something of your work, so it's a part of you. Because your work, Ackerman . . . that's who you are. The things you do to give other people peace and happiness—like Caruso there in *Tosca*—that, *boychekel,* keeps your mind off your troubles, see?

Jake's head, bent way over the table, rested in the palms of his hands. He listened—more to old Izzie than to Caruso.

''You want to quit Hebrew School, go ahead. My s-o-n.'' He dragged the word out in a painful moan. . . . My son the quitter didn't like Caruso. Too fancy, schmansy. You, you want to quit, go ahead. If it was me and I was a believer, I'd do it different. But no one can help you decide.''

The clock clicked loudly as the hands struck eight. Aggie came racing through the door and shoved his time card in just at the *click.* Then Goose and Alex and Jedge followed. *Click-click-click.* Not Harry, though.

Old Izzie waited. But Harry didn't come.

The gluing machine began *whirr*ing. The guys put their aprons on and took up their positions. Each one knew what had to be done. Each one did it.

Old Izzie said, standing by the clock, waiting, ''Some people, some people, see, don't come to work on time. What do they care? Does it mess up *their* time? No. It messes up

**105**

someone else's. That don't mean a thing to some people. People like that, they like empty words. All the Bar Mitzvahs in the world, they don't help people like that.''

He limped over to the cutting machine where a stack of boards for the day's work waited to be trimmed. He set the boards under the long blade, flush with the metal guide on the side, cranked the handle of the cutting machine until the blade was up as high as it would go, and then, with all the muscles and veins of his right arm rippling from the strain, turned the handle until the blade, like a guillotine, sliced through the stack. He lifted the stack of boards—weighing maybe as much as fifty, sixty pounds—to his shoulder, lugged them over to Aggie by the gluing machine, and set them down so that Aggie could place the sheets of marbled paper on the fronts of them for Goose and Jedge to smooth the bubbles out.

It seemed like an elaborate ceremony celebrating some auspicious event, complete with the chanting of Caruso.

As soon as the marble-sheeted boards came towards him, Jake set the leather strips in place on either end and pleated them. Folder between thumb and forefinger of the right hand pressing against the leather being held in place by the forefinger of the left. Pleat. Once. Twice. Three times. Four. Five. Six. Pleat. *Thump* with the blunt-ended hammer. Voilà!

He was into it completely, absorbed by the incredibility of it, of the square-cornered, marble-sheeted board that Goose and the others slipped sideways to him so he could put the rounded, leather-covered strips on either side, and make it become, in—what?—a minute, something whole. A desk pad.

Until the time clock clicked loudly and he looked up and there, at eight-thirty, stood Harry, his shoulders so blithely cocked Jake wanted to vomit.

Nobody said a word.

Not even old Izzie, who shrugged his shoulders, twisted his keg-shaped body until it didn't face Harry anymore, and lumbered off to the embossing room to bring Alex fresh leather strips.

Caruso's voice, sharp and thin as a needle, reached to the sheet-metal ceiling. But Harry didn't care. Those shoulders of his were pulled back anyway.

Jake wanted to poke him right in the mouth.

Not just for coming in late as though it didn't matter; so why shouldn't he? Not just for lying about the damned spitballs; everybody else was throwing them, so what was wrong about his keeping his mouth shut? Jake felt like popping Harry right on the kisser for something else. For ignoring old Izzie's leg, which even Harry's own father was trying, in his own way, to make right, but which Harry, in his way, couldn't or wouldn't.

The leg was there for Harry to see, and Harry didn't even see it. He just came in late, like the whole world was his and he didn't have to care at all about another single person. Even though old Izzie hadn't said yes, and hadn't said no, Jake, seeing Harry traipse in like that, already knew he had to go through with it. He had to get that Bar Mitzvah, no matter what, no matter how much tutoring Harry Katz would have to give him.

He had to for Mama and Papa, first off. But also, now, for old Izzie, who hadn't told him one way or the other what to do.

Because if Jake didn't, he'd never be able to look old Izzie in the eye anymore and, if he did look Harry in the eye again, it would always have to be sideways, out of shame.

# Chapter 19

That's the way the war on the home front—complete with medals—gained momentum.

Not with Medals of Honor.

Not, not with those.

But with gold Bar Mitzvah medals: six-pointed stars pendent from curved bars inscribed in Hebrew with the words *Bar Mitzvah*.

They weren't the same. The president of the United States didn't fly you to Washington, D.C., and the White House to put them around your neck in a ceremony on the White House lawn.

But they'd have to do.

There wasn't anything else.

And the way to earning them was paved with obstacles, beginning with the business of the high-top boots, right after school started again in that fall of 1943, the fall preceding the winter of Harry's Bar Mitzvah.

Mama said, "Boots with a pocketknife? You want to buy boots with a pocketknife? People are being slaughtered all over and that's what you want to buy?"

She meant no harm, of course. No slight. But in the world of her memories, knives had a certain, special purpose. The Cossacks had used them in the nightmare of her growing up; knives—of whatever sort—were forever etched in her mind as despicable, horrifying implements of carnage.

Jake, thinking ahead to the winter already and, maybe even more, to Harry's Bar Mitzvah in December (about which Harry had already said casually one evening—in the middle of tutoring Jake—"My dad's getting me a brand-new suit and a pair of high-top boots for the Bar Mitzvah, and there'll be at least a hundred people coming to see it and afterwards we're having a big party")—Jake fought to convince Mama.

"We've got enough ration coupons for it, Mama," he said. "And . . . and if you want, I'll take the knife out of the pocket and let you keep it. Honest."

It was a lot bigger sacrifice than it sounded—giving up that knife, sheathed so neatly in the slip of a pocket at the top of the boot that it could have been mistaken for a bayonet. But that wasn't important. What was important was the battle for those medals.

"Besides," Jake said, "I've saved up my money from Gold's for it."

Mama didn't have the heart to say no. The air was already filled with the first signs of winter, but she wore the wet towel tight around her forehead nevertheless and chopped liver in the wooden bowl on the table. She shrugged her hunched-over shoulders and relented with a long, deep sigh.

Jake sighed, too. Not out of resignation. Out of relief. Now, at least, he wouldn't have to ask her why, if Max and Michael and Benjy (in the photographs they sent home) wore boots just like the ones he wanted, why shouldn't he?

So with Mama wearily shrugging—what else was a person

to do?—he rushed to the telephone near the stove, dropped a nickel into the slot, and called Harry.

"You want to get high-top boots together?" he said.

Mama, her arm rippling with fat, chopped at the liver, chanting, "God should watch over us." She put all of herself into it, as though she were hacking to pieces all the miseries of her life: the war, the rapacious Cossacks, ration coupons, and even the boots.

"Sure, kiddo," Harry said. "You can come with me when I get mine if you want to."

"Thanks, buddy," Jake said, knowing that pride was evil and that late bloomers couldn't be choosy.

He went to the bedroom, opened his drawer, and took out the fifteen dollars he'd saved from Gold's and counted it and recounted it, his fingers shaking. Fifteen dollars! All his own. Earned by the sweat of his own brow! And now, finally, he'd have the boots, whether it would be summer or not when his Bar Mitzvah came and boots would be too hot to wear.

They went to Simonson's Shoe Store on Division Street to get them.

Jake saw, from the way Harry asked for a pair, that they were just boots to him, plain, simple boots—things to wear with a Bar Mitzvah outfit.

"Here," Harry said when the man brought the box over, "I'll put it on myself." And then he laced one up loosely, so that it was really impossible to get the full effect of the way it looked, his only concern being to get the thing over with as soon as possible.

But for Jake the boots were more. He had to feel them first, lifting each one from the box in the salesman's hand to rub it with his fingers, especially where the pocket for the knife was. Oh, they were more real than the lead soldiers in the cigar box, all right! The boots had no burrs along the edges that a kid could cut his hand on.

All they had was the thick seam along the back and the reflection of the overhead light off the brown leather.

That's what the boots had.

And that's what Jake felt through his fingertips as, with the impatient Harry and the impatient salesman looking on, he caressed the boots.

He had to force himself, finally, to sit down and try them on.

"Let me lace 'em up myself," he told the salesman.

The store was empty, so the salesman nodded.

And Jake pulled the long, brown shoelaces tight through each eyelet and then up to the hooks at the top. When he had tied the bows, he shot up and paraded in front of the mirror, seeing only the boots, the impressiveness of the boots, reflected at a crazy angle in the mirror, as though he were scaling a wall with unsuspecting Nazi guards at the top of it.

"I'll buy them!" he practically shouted, satisfied. More than satisfied. Gleeful, actually, that now, at last, he had part of the uniform.

And he and Harry left the store, each with a box under his arm, and headed to Harry's house for the tutoring session.

Jake marched. He measured each stride carefully so that it equaled Harry's. The shoulders were back, the chest was out, the chin tucked in.

He could feel in his bones now, in the subtle chill of fall creeping up his sleeves, how close he was getting to becoming someone a person could be proud of, with those combat-like boots tucked under his arm, following in Harry's footsteps, doing all the right things or all the things right that had to be done.

He felt good until they reached Harry's house and found Mr. Katz, whom Jake hadn't seen before, waiting for them. In the doorway, yet, with a yarmulke on and his mouth curved up wide in a grin that showed a row of tobacco-stained teeth.

"Hi, sweetheart," Mr. Katz said, wrapping Harry in his arms and hugging him tightly. "Did you get the ones you wanted? Do they match your suit? Do you like them?"

Harry pulled the boots—brown, gleaming—from the box and waved them at his father.

Jake stayed in the background, feeling embarrassed, shifting from leg to leg, waiting.

When Harry finally got around to introducing him, Jake said to Mr. Katz, "How do you do, sir?" expecting that to be all he'd have to say, so they could get inside and begin to study the way they'd been doing before, without Mr. Katz there.

But Mr. Katz wasn't ready to let it die yet. He put his arm around Jake's shoulder, clutched him tight, and with all his tobacco-stained teeth on display, said, "Jacob, I'm glad to meet any friend of my Harry's. I'm glad he brings a friend home."

They went inside with the boots. Mr. Katz, who did not look like the ice-skating type, was still smiling for whatever reason. Through the darkened mustiness, Jake was suddenly aware of all the aspects of the place he hadn't paid attention to before: the cluttered, massed, heaped-up piles of laundry; the dusty bureau; the velvet couch covered with newspapers. The place reeked of tobacco smoke and other more exotic smells that Jake knew came from cooking but not like any cooking he'd ever smelled. Sweet, heavy, almost syrupy.

Jake thought, You can tell Harry's got no mother. That's for sure.

He didn't have anyone else, either, except a grandfather—who stayed locked up in his room studying the *Gemara*.

Mr. Katz kissed Harry on the cheek and sent the two of them off to study.

"Yeah," Harry said, in answer to Jake's first question when they were finally alone, "that's right. Just the three of us. That's why my dad's making such a big Bar Mitzvah for me."

As though the bigness of the Bar Mitzvah was the important thing, more important than the Bar Mitzvah itself. As though the bigness of the Bar Mitzvah made up for the smallness of other things, like Harry's mother's having gone off and his having only a father and a grandfather to live with.

They sat on opposite sides of the bed. The room was lit by one tiny yellow-bulbed lamp. Clothing lay strewn about the floor gathering up motes of dust.

In the dim light, Harry—hunched over on the bed the way he was, with his elbows on his knees and his head resting in the palms of his hands—looked like a clown someone had torn the mask from.

Jake put his boots aside and opened his *Complete Bar Mitzvah Book*.

"Your dad's a nice guy," he said. "He's really friendly."

"Yeah," Harry said.

"You're lucky," Jake said. "I mean, it's nice, his being interested in the boots and stuff." He didn't really think Harry was lucky. And Harry didn't think so either. But neither of them could say it.

# Chapter 20

Every day now, after work and before Hebrew School, they studied together, trading off jokes about who'd make the better speech and who'd chant the reading from the Torah more correctly and who'd say all the blessings flawlessly.

They didn't, either of them, joke about the gold Bar Mitzvah medal and which one of them would wear it more proudly.

They never joked about that.

Days passed. Weeks.

Jake scarcely had time to worry about anything else but the Bar Mitzvahs.

First, Harry's.

Then his own.

The first snows of winter began to whiten the streets and frighten off the people.

Maybe the snows—or their defeat at the Battle of the Fire Extinguisher—had frightened Howie and Gene and Stash off, too.

Because Howie would pass Jake in front of the apartment

and, huddled up in his winter coat with his eyes focused on the snow, he didn't seem to recognize Jake.

Who knew why?

What did it matter?

There were the Bar Mitzvahs. His and Harry's. They were what mattered.

Even more now than before.

Because Papa, when he came home now for dinner, started saying how the war was getting better, that the Allies had begun to turn the tide against the Axis powers, and that there were rumors about how, in the spring, General Eisenhower would lead an invasion of Europe and wouldn't that be fine, with Jake's Bar Mitzvah coming just in time to celebrate the victories that were sure to follow?

Jake's fervor escalated. Papa said that and Mama nodded. It was a sign they wanted the Bar Mitzvah as much as he did.

He bent to the task with doubled effort, rehearsing, whenever he had a free minute, blessings for the wine and the bread and the washing of the hands and the putting on of the prayer shawl and the taking out of the Scrolls from the Holy Ark and putting them back in—he rehearsed each and every blessing, each ritual, with doubled energy and devotion.

Even at the shop, pleating the corners of the desk pads, he practiced to pass the time, making the blessings into a cadenced diversion, much like old Izzie's operas, against which he measured off each pleat.

Blessed art thou, O Lord our God, King of the Universe, who hast chosen us from all peoples, and hast given us thy Law. Blessed art thou, O Lord, giver of the Law.

Pleat. Pleat.

Blessed art thou, O Lord our God, King of the Universe, who hast given us the Law of truth, and hast planted everlasting life in our midst. Blessed art thou, O Lord, giver of the Law.

Pleat. Pleat.

Until one afternoon, when it was dark outside already even though it was only four o'clock and his legs still tingled from the cold walk—he resisted the strong temptation to wear the new boots—from Lafayette to the shop. Jake, immersed in the pleating and the rhythm of the prayers, felt old Izzie's fingers on his shoulders. Jake, startled, dropped his folder. The first thing that came to him was that old Izzie, with his habit of reading minds, was about to scream at him the way he had at Harry for being more interested in Bar Mitzvahs than in making desk pads.

He shriveled under the grip, scarcely daring to look into old Izzie's steely gray eyes.

When he did, he thought—he wasn't sure—he saw a light there, deep in the back of the eyes, darting out at him.

It made him laugh.

Old Izzie laughed, too.

Aggie, shoving a piece of paper through the gluing machine, glanced over his shoulder at the two of them and mumbled something about battle fatigue. He shook his head, as though this kind of insanity was beyond him.

Harry peered at them sideways. He didn't even bother to shake his head.

"What . . . what . . . what's the matter, Mr. Gold?" Jake asked, his own laugh reaching towards hysteria.

Old Izzie beckoned to him. "Come over to the desk, Ackerman. I show you something."

Jake timidly eyed the others, wanting to shrug the whole

thing off, as if to say, "Hey, buddies. It's nothing, so don't go getting any ideas." But something in the crook of old Izzie's beckoning finger pushed his laughter beyond control.

His body shook with it as he followed old Izzie to the desk, where the old man stood pointing to a letter.

The damned thing looked exactly like the letters Max and Michael and Benjy had gotten, inviting them to Serve Their Country.

Jake stopped laughing as abruptly as he'd begun.

He looked at the letter more closely.

Now, mesmerized by it, he saw it came from the staff of a United States general.

Old Izzie's keg-shaped body shook in its own hysteria.

"We, Ackerman," he proclaimed in broken excitement, "we are making a special desk pad for a general in the United States Army. Do you hear that? A letter saying, Please make such and such a desk pad for our general."

Jake's nose rubbed against old Izzie's shoulder. He leaned in so close to him, his nose touched old Izzie's shirt.

A letter from a general's headquarters?

An invitation to Gold, Inc., Chicago, Illinois, to make a desk pad for an officer of the United States Army?

"Jesus!" Jake whistled. It was, of course, not a good whistle. But it was the best he could do. "Wow, Mr. Gold!"

The *real* war had come, not just to Crystal Square and the shop, but to him as well.

Because old Izzie had said "we." Not "me." Not "the company." But "we"—you and me.

And Jake wasn't even thirteen yet.

"Can I . . . When do we . . . Holy cow!" Jake stammered.

The thing he tried, he wanted, to say needed no finishing. Old Izzie finished it for him. "The cat ain't got your tongue no more, eh? You want to know when we begin, eh? Well, Ackerman. We begin today. Right now.''

Jake moved to grab old Izzie. But then he remembered the others at the table and pulled back. Shy, ashamed, he pulled back and swallowed.

The grunts from the table became louder. Jake turned. He saw them all—Harry especially—with long faces and he knew what each of them—Harry especially—was thinking: Ass licker! Goddamn boss's pet!

He had an urge to run over to Harry and apologize. It doesn't mean nothing, buddy. You're still Top Sergeant. Honest to pete!

But then he wanted to take another long look at the letter, to memorize it, right down to the signature, so he could tell Mama and Papa about it.

But he stood there, next to old Izzie, and didn't do anything. Not really. He was afraid to. Afraid of the grunts and afraid to yell out, ''Sure thing, Mr. Gold!'' Even though the yell was bursting inside him.

Harry would have a fit.

Harry would know. He'd know Jake was making up for the bad leg that nobody else was making up for.

Jake couldn't stand it.

Not with Harry's tutoring him. Not with Harry's extinguishing the hell out of the triumvirate.

''Can Harry, Mr. Gold . . . Can the other guys help, too?''

He was practically pleading, facing into old Izzie's steely gray eyes with that dart of light coming out from inside them, meaning every word.

Harry chortled. Loud, piercingly. As if . . . as if *he* knew better. Like *he* had some special pipeline right into Jake's head and knew—don't kid him—that Jake was lying through

**118**

his goddamn teeth and didn't want any of them—especially not Harry—to get into this act. No sirree!

It felt like a panzer attack. Whichever way Jake moved, it seemed like he was cornered.

He didn't try again, not with Harry making a big joke out of it.

It wouldn't have made a difference anyway. Whether because old Izzie heard the laughter too and knew what it meant or because he'd already made his mind up anyway, he held out that letter and waved it at Jake and said, "This is a two-man job, Ackerman. I do the cutting; you do the pleating."

At least he didn't say anything about botching.

Thank God, he didn't say anything about botching.

Harry, at least, wouldn't be able to hold that against Jake too.

# Chapter 21

During the weeks before Christmas and Harry's Bar Mitzvah, Jake and old Izzie worked hard on the special desk pad.

Jake was so euphoric that one day on his way from Lafayette to the shop, he stopped at Casarrella's School and Novelty Store, on Cortez, stared at the four-starred flags for sale in the window, and went into the store, took out some money and bought one, thinking he'd present it to Mama—as a lark, of course—when he went home that night. Just for kicks. Just to make her laugh a little to see how her baby was growing up.

But the minute he got outside, he wondered if it was a mistake. Mama might turn it into a crisis. Even though the war was going better now and the V-letters were coming home steadily enough for her and Papa to have made a big stack of them right next to the photographs on the mantelpiece, what did she need another crisis for?

So he crumpled it up and when nobody was watching, tossed it behind a garbage can in the alley and raced into the shop, right over to the table near the cutting machine old

Izzie had set aside for the two of them to work at, and buried himself in the action, joining old Izzie, who was already cutting out the paper patterns he used to guide him in shaping the leather.

They worked without words, the tenor voice of Tagliavini accompanying their movements: the snick of the scissors, the scratch of the leather knives, the bang of the hammers, smooth flowing and rhythmic.

The roll of leather from which the pad was to be made was maroon and pebbly-grained, and each time old Izzie got ready to cut out a piece, placing the paper pattern on top of it as a guide, he pursed his thick lips tightly together as though intently praying. These were not now, as with the regular pads, to be just strips of leather. These were to be overlapping leaves, file dividers, on either side of the huge pad with the four stars of a general on them. These had to be done just right, so the general could file papers under each leaf and still be able to see the edge of the next leaf below with its clear plastic slot for a label.

It took a lot of prayer to get them exactly the way they ought to be.

Jake didn't mind. The more prayer it took, the more engrossed he got, the less he worried about Harry, always there at the table by the green window, a silent vigilante.

Old Izzie said, "The damned leaves, they'll be hard to glue without the seams showing, so they look like pages in a book."

Jake nodded. The thing had to look as though it had been "born" like a single thing, not made.

That was the secret. No matter how hard, how painstaking, you needed to work at it so that when it was finished, there was no question about it. That *was* the way, the only way it could be. There couldn't be any other way for it to look.

So that the general, seeing it, would say, "Now, there. That's the way a desk pad should be."

He didn't need to see seams and joints, with seeped-out, congealed globs of glue showing how it had been put together.

"He don't need to know," old Izzie kept murmuring. "That's all. Final. Kaput."

Jake understood.

The trouble was, doing it right left Harry out of it, and the more Harry was left out of it, the more it gnawed at Jake. And the more it gnawed at him, the more he found himself thinking, as the afternoon wore on, Poor Harry. Jesus Christ! Poor Harry.

He eyed him more often, though Harry didn't seem to be giving him any reason to, sitting there silent but vigilant, along with the others at the table.

Jake, in fact, began to think about Harry nearly as much as he worried about whether the pad was working out right, the way old Izzie and the general would want it to.

Harry sat there, resigned.

Until it occurred to Jake that Harry—not Jake or anybody else for that matter—should have been working with old Izzie on this pad. He should have been having all the glory to begin with.

And that's when Jake leaped up from his stool, plunked the sticky, white bone folder down on the table, and stretched and yawned—it was one of the best yawns he'd ever faked— and said to old Izzie, "Geez, Mr. Gold. I don't know why, but I'm really tired."

Old Izzie looked up from the paper patterns he was snipping out with the scissors. "So?" he said.

"Can't Harry take my place for a while?" Jake said.

His body surged with a powerful satisfaction. He imagined himself returning from a successful reconnaissance mission deep in enemy territory, reporting to his commanding officer and getting that slap of pleasure on the back that meant more than all the words in the world.

Old Izzie's jowls twitched.

"Ackerman," he said, "go home maybe. Maybe you're coming down with a cold. Go home. Rest."

He didn't say a word about Harry. He wouldn't even look his way.

Jake couldn't just run over to Harry and spill it all out to him, tell him what a shitty way that was for old Izzie to act. He wanted to. He was dying to.

But he couldn't. The reconnaissance mission had turned into one big flop.

He sank back onto the stool. No wonder he'd thrown away the four-starred flag. Something in him must have known all along it was wrong, his thinking he deserved to be a star along with the other three when anybody could see he was nothing.

He bent back to the pleating. It had all been a mistake, including the high-top boots. He banged the pleats harder. He should have been helping Harry, not the other way around. Pleat, pleat. *Bang.* He stared at old Izzie, with the cigar stump in the corner of his mouth, cementing the clear plastic label holder to the bottom of each leaf of the pad. Pleat, pleat. *Bang, bang.*

Poor Harry. Some buddy he's got!

Poor Harry. The guy hasn't even got a mother!

Poor Harry. And he didn't even have to tutor me if he didn't want to!

And so it went, until everybody started punching out.

All the excitement of helping old Izzie with the special desk pad fizzled. *P-f-f-t.*

How could you make everything into something when you didn't have anything to make it with?

When you were absolutely nothing?

The shame of it overwhelmed Jake. When he got outside, standing on the step by the green door, staring after Harry who was heading towards Hebrew School and seemed to be leaving him behind, Jake screamed, "I'll come over and help you with your Bar Mitzvah, too, Harry. I'll come over early Saturday morning and help you get ready. Okay?"

It came out before he knew what he was saying. It came out even before he knew why he was saying it.

Harry stopped in the snow. The wind whistled past his up-turned collar as he turned, statutesque as always. Stiff as the wind itself.

All he said was, "Okay. Yeah. Sure. If you want." And he kept on walking, leaving Jake to catch up—to walk behind him, repentant, silent, long-faced. Dying for another chance.

One more chance, that's all.

That's all it would take.

He could live up to his part of that blood oath which hadn't even been sworn to but which was as good as one that had been, anyway.

Only when they reached Hebrew School, Harry murmured one other thing, barely audible above the whistling wind.

"My ma and her new husband are coming to see me. So you'll have to come over at five-thirty. That way there'll be time to practice."

Jake couldn't hold it back.

He slapped Harry hard on the back. "You bet, buddy.

We'll rehearse your speech and everything. You'll wow 'em.''

If that wasn't the sealing of a pact, he'd be damned!

If that wasn't making everything into something, nothing was.

# Chapter 22

But who was supposed to know that the first blizzard of the winter would hit the Friday night before Harry's Bar Mitzvah?

Who could have known it?

Without that storm, things might have turned out differently. Without it, Harry might have been a buddy still.

But it stormed. God, did it storm!

The snow fell so heavily, the wind blew so fiercely, that when Jake started polishing his high-top boots that night, Mama had a fit.

"What kind of arrangement," she said, "what kind of plan is it to go at five o'clock in the morning to a Harry Katz's house to help him get ready for a Bar Mitzvah? Who ever heard of such a thing? In the middle of a snowstorm yet, too? It's craziness," she said. "Three sons have to live in the snow in Europe with the Nazis, and now another one has got to do the same thing in Chicago? For someone else's Bar Mitzvah? I never heard of such a thing in my whole life."

Jake polished the boots anyway. What was the point of trying to explain? She wouldn't, she couldn't, understand, never having had to deal with Bar Mitzvahs before. If he told her he was supposed to get to Harry's house by five-thirty and then knock on the window four times so he could let Harry know he was there without waking up Harry's father and grandfather, she'd only wonder why.

"It's nothing, Mama," he said. "Harry Katz doesn't live far away." A lie, but so what? She didn't need to know Harry lived eight blocks away. It was enough she knew her last son hadn't ever been outside that early in his life. Never mind that there were five inches of snow on the ground already and no signs of relief.

Well, the boots would help. And the mackinaw. With any kind of luck, there'd be enough shine left on the boots after the hike so that Jake wouldn't look like a total idiot when everybody started piling into the synagogue at nine, dressed to kill.

He swished the brush across the boots several more times until they shone like old man Gold's head. "Please don't worry, okay, Mama? I'll go to sleep at nine o'clock and won't wake you up, and I'll come home right after the Bar Mitzvah."

She fretted her brows; she paced back and forth the length of the whole kitchen. It was too much for her.

But Jake had to do it. Not just because he'd promised it, but because . . . well, to make everything into something—isn't that what old Izzie said?

When the boots were done and he'd set them right at the foot of the bed where he'd be able to find them in the dark without stumbling over everything, Jake put his mackinaw on the chair near the dresser. He even folded his pants neatly to keep the crease sharp.

He set the alarm for four-thirty, his hands trembling slightly at the meaning of it all, of his actually having—

finally having—a rendezvous with destiny, like his brothers.

He got into his pajamas, went back out into the kitchen to kiss Mama good night, promised her he'd be all right, then locked himself in the bedroom so he couldn't see the three stars in the window, and sat in the dark watching the snow drift down past the streetlight near the telephone pole Chris had fallen from.

The street, as though it had a premonition that worse things than Chris's fall were possible, was still as death.

Jake climbed into bed but couldn't fall asleep. He kept checking the alarm clock, but every time he looked up at it, its hands seemed not to have moved.

He turned his head from one side of the pillow to the other, but that didn't help. He said the Bar Mitzvah prayers over and over, the ones he'd be helping Harry rehearse in the morning; the very ones he'd be saying aloud himself in six months, not in the grandiose Galician Congregation's synagogue, but in Hannah Rachel's smaller, more modest Bell Avenue Synagogue.

By nine-thirty, when he heard Papa tramping in, stomping the snow from his galoshes, Jake had already said the *Shema*: "Hear, O Israel, the Lord our God, the Lord is One."

One hundred times. He'd repeated each of the blessings he knew . . . for wine and bread and water . . . a score of times.

Mama's and Papa's muted voices carried easily through the door of the bedroom, but they did not deter Jake—except when Papa wondered too loud if the boys were having such a terrible winter in Europe, too. Jake tried a new tack. He imagined the general—upon receiving the desk pad Jake and old Izzie had put together with their own hands—being so happy with it that he sent for the two of them to award them

Medals of Honor and to parade them in front of his troops.

That nearly worked. That nearly brought Jake's eyes to a close, but then he got to thinking about how poor Harry, right at this very moment when he, Jake, was having these gigantic delusions of grandeur, was probably having a conniption fit worrying about how it would seem to everybody to have his mother and her new husband at the Bar Mitzvah, along with his father and his grandfather.

That brought Jake up short. He propped himself up on his elbow.

"Shit!" he swore softly. "What a damned crappy thing for the two of them to do to him!"

The clock ticked away to ten and to eleven. Four-thirty in the morning got closer and closer and still he couldn't fall asleep. The slit of light coming in from under the bedroom door went out, and his head spun. Would the blizzard stop people from getting to the Bar Mitzvah? And would Harry, having worked so hard, be let down if they didn't come?

So it went, Jake didn't know for how many more hours. Maybe he dozed; maybe he slept a little. Otherwise, why would the alarm, in the pitch-black night, finally have rung when he least expected it to, startling him so that he flailed his arms, nearly knocking the clock over, wanting to stop it before it woke Mama and Papa up?

His eyes, at first, refused to stay open. They sagged, pulling him back down to the soft, warm, hollowed-out pillow.

But the echo of the alarm nagged at him. There was no getting around it. It was the morning of Harry's Bar Mitzvah, and Harry—poor Harry—probably having been up all night, waited for him.

Jake yawned a huge yawn; his jaws cracked. He managed somehow to get his legs over the bed, but they froze there.

**129**

The radiators were only now beginning to hiss with steam. The heat gurgling up through the pipes sorely tempted him to plop right back down to sleep. But then a glimmer of light seeped through the window, between the shade and the sill. It silhouetted the shiny high-top boots.

He leaped out of bed. It was four-thirty and he had eight blocks to go. In the middle of the night yet. A rendezvous with destiny. Like every other grown-up, patriotic American.

He was going to do his duty, by God!

Seeing more with his hands than with his eyes, he groped for the sharply creased trousers; somehow got into them, one goose-bumpy leg after the other; then into the starched, white dress shirt, whose sleeves buttoned just above his wristbones and turned his arms, when he let them dangle their full length, into boards.

The last things to go on were the boots.

He handled them gingerly, cautiously. Like the boots of combat soldiers all over the world, they required special treatment, a caressing tenderness to prepare them for the elements.

When he had laced them their entire length, fumbling against each eyelet in the darkness, he lifted the pocketknife from the pocket and fondled it a final time. For the memory of it, for something to sustain him against the hostility waiting outside. He gripped it tightly for a moment, reluctant to yield it up to the top of the dresser.

But promises were promises. He gave it up with a soft *thud* to the dresser top.

He put on his hand-me-down mackinaw, his cap, his gloves, his long woolen scarf.

Now, at nearly five o'clock, he was ready, eager almost, to meet the universe, to grapple with the elements.

Until, having stolen through the door and down the stairs like a commando penetrating deep into enemy territory, he encountered the first taste of the bitter, snowy morning.

It was like running into a frozen, steel wall.

The wind, even on the front-porch landing, bit into his cheeks and his lips, so that before he took a step, he had to wrap the scarf around his face, leaving only his eyes exposed.

The street was incredibly still. Everything was white. The snow, in the light of the streetlamps, flickered brilliantly.

Jake began to crunch, to smush his way through the ankle-deep snow, north on Francisco, fully awake now, icily up now, his eyes tearing from the wind that wrapped itself around the barren branches of the trees and twisted them, creaked them into such grotesque shapes, he had to raise his collar around his neck to stop from seeing them.

There were no cars; there were no horns; there was no *squish*ing of tires.

Once, near Division and California, he saw the far-off, miniscule circle of light from the California Avenue streetcar and, moments later, heard the *clang* of its bell.

But that was all.

Otherwise, it was just the two of them—Jacob Ackerman and the blizzard—pitted against each other.

Jake didn't mind.

He knew what he had to do. He knew where he had to go. He knew how much someone was depending on him.

He bucked the wall of the icy wind and crunched through the snow. Once he made it to California and began heading east, he felt a little safer. There were streetlights. And though there were more shadows, too, that danced, it seemed, in the wind, at least they were in front of him and he didn't need to constantly peer over the top of his upturned collar and over his shoulder to see where the shadows came from and whether they needed fearing.

His hands—gloved, stiff—were shoved deep into the mackinaw's slash pockets. They tingled with the cold. So did his legs, despite the high-top boots. With each step, the boots sunk deep into the snow. With each step, the muscles of his body tightened to raise the legs up and out of the snow. His thighs burned. But there was no doing anything about that. He couldn't very well pull his hands out of his pockets to rub the thighs warm.

By the time he reached Washtenaw and Division, his breath was coming fast and heavy, in raspy, steamy sounds that pounded out of him from the depths of his chest. A sweat broke out under the woolen ice-skating cap, and he was afraid it might freeze, gluing the cap to his forehead forever. But there was nothing to do about that either.

The last block was the worst.

Maybe because the shadows had fiercer angles to them. Maybe because the snow-heavy tree branches creaked more loudly and the two-story houses, in the stillness of the morning, were more ghoulish looking.

Jake snapped his head from side to side, studying the street in frenzied, feverish movements.

He couldn't let some trench-coated, broadbrim-hatted counter-espionage agent dart out at him from the shadowed recess of a porch or alleyway and grab him, half nelson, and strangle him right there on the spot, where his body would sink in the snow and stay buried all winter long without anybody—Mama or Papa or Harry or old Izzie—knowing where he'd disappeared to.

He couldn't.

A branch cracked to his left, just opposite the building next to Harry's. Jake jumped. Leaped, actually, completely out of the snow. He ran so fast—those remaining ten, fifteen, twenty feet to Harry's concrete steps—and bounded up those eight steps with such a rush, he couldn't believe, when he got there, that he had.

He simply, when he got to the landing and the window, came to an abrupt stop, like a spent shell dropping at the end of its trajectory. Numb. Frozen. Dead. Scared stiff.

He gasped for breath, for his lungs to fill up with air again. The breath came out of his mouth, through the scarf, in a vapor.

Well, the vapor, at least, meant he was still alive. That was something. He was at Harry's house and he was alive. And when he looked at his watch, it was five-thirty. Exactly.

So he'd made it after all.

And now he tapped on the living-room window, waiting for Harry's face to pop up from behind the curtains.

Nothing.

He tapped again, a little bit—not much—louder.

Nothing.

He stomped softly in the snow to bring life back to his legs. He checked his watch again. Maybe there had been a mistake. Maybe the watch was running fast.

He tapped once more, louder.

There was no face in the window—warm, serene, protected from the cold or otherwise—popping up to greet him.

Damn! he thought. What do I do now?

Harry must have gone to the bathroom, that's what. So Jake gave it another minute, counting to one hundred twenty, slowly, shifting from one leg to the other to keep warm.

One hundred nineteen. One hundred twenty.

He rapped on the window again, four raps this time. Four loud raps this time.

All he could think of was that there wouldn't be time to help Harry and that he'd made a stupid, blundering mistake, mixed things up.

I've screwed him up for good, that's what I've done.

He checked the address above the door and wondered whether he even had the right house. He went down to the sidewalk again and checked the houses on either side.

It was the right place, all right. No doubt about that.

So why didn't Harry answer?

He rapped and rapped and rapped. He paced back and forth, just to keep warm.

He began to leave. He went back. He began to leave. He went back.

And then he decided—his ears frozen by now and his high-top boots soaking wet—he decided to try one last time.

This time he banged on the window, his nose pressed up tight to it so that if there was any movement inside at all, any sign of life, he'd catch it and plead with it to let him in, for pete's sake, before he froze to death.

This time, emerging from the inner darkness, something, someone, stirred, edged its way ever so slowly towards the window.

Jake couldn't be sure who, what it was, it moved so sluggishly, so lackadaisically.

That . . . that can't be Harry, Jake thought. He ought to be . . . He'd be running if it was.

His nose froze to the window. He pulled back an inch or two to rub it with his gloved hand. Waiting. Not understanding. Hoping.

Until the face—yes, it was Harry's!—sleepily peered back at him, yawning, signaling with a feeble jerk to come in.

Jake did. An icicle slithering into the heat of the black apartment, dripping with sweat.

Harry was still in his pajamas.

Harry wasn't even fully awake.

"What . . . what happened, Harry?" Jake whispered.

"What . . . what did you say?" Harry grumbled.

He didn't even wait to hear an answer. Hunched over, stooped, rubbing his belly, he turned his back on Jake and led the way to the bedroom.

Once they got there, once he hopped back into bed under the warmth of the blanket, Harry said, "I forgot. I forgot to set my alarm clock. Anyway, there's plenty of time yet."

# Chapter 23

Jake couldn't wait. He couldn't wait for the damned thing to be over and done with. For all the people in their pretty clothes to stop oohing and ahing about what a wonderful boy Harry was, wasn't he? And wasn't that a wonderful speech he gave—wasn't it?—about what it meant, finally, to be a good Jew? And wasn't it wonderful that today, finally, he was a man? (And maybe a fountain pen as well?)

Rabbi Shonfeld practically kissed Harry, that's what he did, right there in public petting his little Katzele up on the platform by the altar.

Jake wanted to vomit. But he was too tired to, too pooped out and shivery all over from the hike. Besides, there were things to do yet.

He waited around long enough to shake Harry's hand and say "Congratulations, Harry," even though what he meant was, "So long, kiddo." No "buddy" now. No foxhole sergeant who needed a little looking up to, with all those stripes and authority. Not after a hike through a blizzard for absolutely no good reason except to ruin—absolutely destroy—the high-top boots.

Storm or no storm, Jake fled from the Galician Congregation synagogue. Not knowing where. Not knowing how. Just fleeing, trying to noodle things through.

Whether to drop out of Hebrew School—the blessings didn't mean anything anyhow; they were empty words—or to punch Howie Woscowicz in the mouth once and for all or what.

Because now it was down to the wire. There wasn't anything left to latch on to. All there was left to show for a nightmare like that was a pair of soggy boots that not even a brand-new pocketknife could bring the life back to.

Jake slushed through the streets for an hour, watching the plows on the fronts of the North Avenue trolleys make wedge-shaped paths over the tracks so that the trolleys that followed wouldn't have it so hard; stopping near the library on North and California, to see how long it took the man in his long woolen coat to shovel the snow from the sidewalk, and then feeling guilty that the man was working so hard while he—Jake Ackerman—stood by merely watching. He headed even farther west along North Avenue, entering Humboldt Park right near the barely recognizable—because it was so covered with snow—statue of Kosciusko, the Pole who fought side by side with General Washington during the Revolution; and plodding through the snowdrifts over to Bunker Hill, where kids all bundled up tore down the slope on sleds.

Somehow or other, he ended up in front of the shop, standing by the green glass door, hands on hips, staring through the scratches in the window the way he had so long ago, hoping now that old Izzie, by some miracle, would be in there alone.

To help him with the noodling, with the new thing that had to be done, now that Harry Katz couldn't be counted on to do it with.

He heard the music—soft and delicate—before he saw old Izzie. A woman's high-pitched voice rising up and up with each note, stretching to the sky.

Old Izzie was at the table with his eyes shut. His hand clutched at the thigh of the bad leg.

Jake opened the door softly and crept into the shop. Faint traces of the smell of glue hit him first. Then the heat of the place crept through the mackinaw.

Jake unbuttoned it and took off his cap and moved to the desk and waited.

Despite the hand that clutched the thigh, old Izzie—his jowls without that twisted tautness—was tranquil, freed from pain by the music.

Jake waited. He couldn't bring himself to disturb him.

It would have been sacrilegious.

He began swaying to the music himself, the way some of the old men in the synagogue swayed when they prayed in their prayer shawls. And as he swayed, thoughts of Harry and the soggy boots drifted from his head.

It was the music now. That was all. And the lovely, delicious heat creeping into him, thawing out the iciness of the long morning.

When the record on the Victrola stopped spinning with a flourish of trumpets and the thunderous, staccato clashing of cymbals, old Izzie's eyes opened. He took his hand from his leg and placed it, with the other hand, on his belly. He stared at the peeling green plaster on the wall behind the table and smiled.

He didn't turn his head.

He said, "I'm glad you came in out of the blizzard." He raised himself from the stool and beckoned Jake to follow him. He limped over to the table near the cutting machine where the general's desk pad was. He pointed to the completed pad. "So," he said, "what do you think, Ackerman? Did we do a job or did we do a job?"

Jake ran his fingers over the pebbly-grained leather, over the pleated and tamped-down corners.

The pad felt like a part of him, like it belonged to him and he to it.

"Yes sir, Mr. Gold," he said. "We sure did!"

He bent over it again, this time running his fingers along the edges, feeling for excess glue.

There wasn't any. The thing was like a work of art.

"When is he going to get it?" Jake said.

"Monday," old Izzie said. "So we got it done in time. Now we pray the general likes it."

Jake said, "He will, Mr. Gold. It looks great."

Old Izzie put an arm around him. "Now," he said, "now you tell me why you come in on a Saturday, eh? You, a Bar Mitzvah boy, coming in on Saturday?"

With the arm—warm, gentle—around his shoulder, Jake said, "I don't think Harry Katz is coming back anymore, Mr. Gold. He was Bar Mitzvahed this morning."

"So," old Izzie said, "tell me something new."

There was nothing new for Jake to tell him except, "I might be able to work more hours after school starting after Christmas."

Old Izzie went over to his chair and plopped down into it. He put another record on and said, "Arias by Tagliavini. Such a voice!" The record began to spin; the rich tenor voice began to fill the shop. Izzie looked up at Jake and whispered, "Where you going to get so much time all of a sudden, what with studying for the Bar Mitzvah?"

"I'm thinking of quitting," Jake said. "It doesn't mean anything anyway."

At first, old Izzie didn't seem to hear. He thumped the

desk top with his fingertips. But as the voice of Tagliavini momentarily disappeared behind a flurry of instruments, he said, "It's a thing a person has to decide himself. Nobody can help with it."

"That's what you said before." Jake laughed. "That's what you said before when the rabbi used the ruler."

What he wanted was for old Izzie to say more, like "Sure! Okay! You can work as many hours as you want." What he wanted was for old Izzie to say, "Bar Mitzvahs aren't for me either."

But it was Saturday and the shop was officially closed, so old Izzie didn't need, maybe, to say anything. Maybe, on Saturdays, he rested from talking, period.

"What I think," old Izzie said when the record stopped, "is that if a person starts something, it's nice if he finishes it. Then he's not left with nothing. Then he knows it's over and it's behind him. He doesn't have to worry about it anymore. People spend all their time worrying. What's left for doing?"

Jake started to go. He buttoned up the mackinaw. Mama would be worried. "I better go home," he said, stealing a final glance at the general's desk pad.

Old Izzie looked him straight in the eye. "Katz doesn't work no more, it's not the end of the world." He thumped harder on the desk. "You'll find other friends, Ackerman. But to give up a Bar Mitzvah for him? Pshaw! What'll you have left?"

Jake was too tired to think, let alone answer. "I'll be in Monday, Mr. Gold," he said.

And he left.

# Chapter 24

The first thing Mama did when he got home was check him for a fever.

"That's all I need," she said, "is for you to get sick."

She ran him into the bedroom and piled blankets on him to keep him from catching pneumonia and brought in one cup of hot tea after another—laced with honey, of course—until Jake dreamed he was drowning.

"I'm fine, Mama, really. I'm fine," he said over and over again, even though he really felt miserable, aching down to the bone, burning from the ankles up.

She relented at last, after planting one final temperature-gauging kiss on his forehead—"Just to be sure"—and let him collapse into a sweaty, obliterating sleep.

And while he slept, he dreamed a frenzied, feverish dream. Snow—tons of white snow—had fallen on the roof over the bedroom, tearing a hole in it large enough for para-troopers with chutes fully open to drop through. He was in bed, but, for some reason, already dressed, and Mama called out to him to go to Weinberg's for groceries. He didn't want to go, but she kept calling out to him that he had to because if he didn't, the store would close and they would all starve to death. He got up but because the snow had caved the roof in, he looked like a snowman and didn't want to be seen like that in public. He yelled out to Mama that she ought to go herself, it was too hard for him to move.

When Mama came to the door and saw that he was covered with snow, she screamed out, but not exactly what Jake expected her to scream. She screamed, "Go anyway, my baby. Otherwise, we'll die of hunger." So Jake, looking at her quizzically, left the room, dragging one heavy step after another, wondering why she would send him out in the storm, especially when the roof needed fixing and everybody knew there was enough food in the house to last a week. Just as he got to the outside door, a figure in a helmet, wielding a bayonet, darted out of the shadows and struck at him. It was only after they finished grappling with each other and Jake had the helmeted one on the ground that he saw who it was. The person he'd beaten up was, of all people, himself.

He woke with a start in a pool of sweat, with his pillow on the floor and his body stretched diagonally across the bed.

He knew he had to get up right that minute and hunt out Howie.

The idea flashed in on him with a dazzling brilliance.

He dressed and left the bedroom, stopping at the living-room window long enough to straighten the white flag with the three stars on it because the flag hung lopsided. Mama, in the kitchen stirring steamy chicken soup in the big black pot on the stove, shrieked when she saw him.

"Jacob," she said, "why did you get up? All that non-sense this morning, you should stay in bed before you catch pneumonia."

"I have to go downstairs to the Woscowiczes', Mama," Jake said. "I need to see Howie about something."

The steam from the pot condensed on the kitchen window and froze in symmetrical crystals that crept upwards over the entire pane. Jake, delirious with fever, ran to the window and began scratching through the ice with his fingernail, etching a heart with an arrow though it and, above that, his initials. He couldn't think of anyone else's initials to add to his, so he left it alone.

Mama went on stirring the soup, staring into the pot, murmuring, without interrupting the rhythm of the hand that clutched the long, wooden spoon, "Don't make trouble with him, Jacob. Pogroms here in Chicago like the ones in Poland we don't need."

Jake kissed the back of her neck that looked like a stubbled chin.

"There won't be any trouble, Mama," he said.

She nodded, kept on stirring, slowly, lugubriously, and stared blankly into the bubbling pot. "Who has any worry left?" she said. "Even worry . . . even worry a person can run out of."

Jake knew she didn't mean it, that she still had enough worry left to last at least through the end of World War II when, hopefully, her three other sons would come home whole and healthy.

He wiped the sweat from his forehead. "Mama," he said, "you'll never stop worrying. It's the way you are." He was ready to let it go at that, when a final thing to say occurred to him. "But if a person keeps on worrying, there's no time left to do other things."

With that, he moved down the carpeted front stairway like a sleepwalker, snippets of his dream mingling with thoughts about Howie, making each step down an excruciating, tormenting exercise.

He didn't know what he was going to say or why. He just stumbled down, shoved by the dream and the fever.

All he could think of was being pissed on all that time ago, and how heavy the roof and the snow caving in on him felt, and that he was too tired to go out and get groceries and too tired to fight helmeted enemies who darted out at him from shadows.

His clenched fist hung in the air ready to rap on Howie's door.

It should have been such an easy thing to do. A knock like any other knock.

But the fist hung frozen in the air.

He was burning up inside and freezing outside, all at the same time.

If I don't do something, he thought, I'll die here, for pete's sake, and nobody'll know.

He heard the echo of the *rap-rap-rap* before he understood that he'd actually done it—hit the door until the knuckles of his fist ached.

It was too late now to turn back upstairs and hide under the blankets.

Howie Woscowicz, with his black, peg-legged pants, stood there staring at him wide-eyed.

Jake's head spun. His eyes stung from the fever. Howie no longer looked like Howie to him.

"What do you want, Ackerman?" Howie said.

Jake stared at him stupidly, struggling to dredge up the words that he knew he'd come downstairs to say but that he just couldn't think of.

"I . . . I . . ." he stammered.

**144**

Howie stood there absolutely still, his hands in his pockets.

Jake hoped he wouldn't hold the fire-extinguisher battle against him.

"It wasn't right, Howie," he said, "using that fire extinguisher. We were at the top of the stairs. You guys weren't."

Howie's mouth sagged.

"What?" he said. "What are you talking about?"

It was a good question. Jake didn't know the answer.

He must have smiled. He wasn't sure. It felt like a smile; the lips felt like they were turned up. But he wasn't sure.

"I . . . I . . ." He tried again. "If . . . you want, Howie," he said, "if you want . . ." He stopped again. He felt embarrassed. Suppose, if he went ahead and asked, suppose Howie called him kike again? But the words in his head had a will of their own. They surged forward despite his embarrassment. "If you want," he went on, "you can come to my Bar Mitzvah in June." He paused for a breath before adding, "It's going to be a small one without a party or lots of people."

Howie scratched his head.

Then *he* began to stammer.

"Well . . . uh . . . I . . . I didn't know you were . . . Geez, Ackerman . . . no kidding."

"If . . . you . . . want to . . ." Jake said.

"Yeah . . . well . . . I'll see, Ackerman. Okay?"

Jake felt himself nodding. His head kept going up and down.

"June, Howie," he said. "It's in June."

He withdrew and climbed upstairs.

Mama was at the door waiting for him, her arms outstretched.

"I'm sick, Mama," Jake said. "I think I'll go back to bed."

"Oy vey!" she shrieked. "I knew. I knew it was pneumonia. You had to go out in a storm for someone else's Bar Mitzvah and get pneumonia?"

Jake reeled into bed.

Things went that way sometimes. What was a person to do?

# Chapter 25

The pneumonia passed, as things like that do.

The hours, the days, the weeks passed.

And Jake's head cleared, enough for him not so much to regret the delirious invitation to Howie as to wonder whether Howie would remember it.

He worked for the Bar Mitzvah now. For it and the medal—the gold, six-pointed Bar Mitzvah medal. Not because of the medal itself anymore, to be worn side by side with Harry's, like two soldiers on parade. But for another reason. He already knew what he had to do with the medal, now that Harry was gone.

He didn't know he'd end up doing what he had to do with it the way—under the circumstances—he actually came to do it. All he knew was what he wanted to do with that medal.

When the first week of June 1944 came and his Bar Mitzvah was less than a week off, he never in his life would have believed that what did happen could have happened: the Allied forces—thousands of men and ships and planes—invaded Normandy with the idea of vanquishing the Nazis and the Japanese and totalitarianism once and for all.

All the papers screamed it out in headlines:

D DAY—ALLIES INVADE NORMANDY

It was like a harbinger, an omen, that so mobilized Jake, he could scarcely sleep that whole week.

Mama and Papa talked about nothing else. They clapped their hands. They danced. Mama's eyes lit up as they hadn't lit up since the beginning of the war; she raised them heavenward and thanked God from morning to night.

All the starred flags—blue and gold alike—in all the windows of Francisco Avenue gleamed intensely and hopefully for the first time in two-and-a-half years.

Old Izzie danced around the shop, too—the best way he could with only one good leg. He sang, in his falsetto, every aria from every opera he liked, making up words when he didn't know them, which was often.

The machines *whirr*ed; the glue smelled warm and sweet. Now, though, the *whirr*ing seemed livelier; the smell seemed sweeter.

Jedge and Goose and Aggie, for the first time, began humming along as old Izzie sang.

If anyone missed Harry, no one said anything.

Least of all Jake, who, when he thought about Harry at all, thought about him as someone might think of a deserter, a guy who acts tough while the going's easy, but who, when the going gets tough, runs.

Jake felt sorry for him, that's all. Sorry that he couldn't have stuck it out—on the morning of the snowstorm first; at Gold, Inc., second.

Because, frankly, it would have been great to have someone come over early on the Saturday of his own Bar Mitzvah to help him rehearse so he wouldn't make a fool of himself.

It would have been nice to have someone help with the speech Papa had written: the Yiddish speech which—Jake had to admit it—he didn't understand in the least; the English speech which—he was ashamed to admit—he understood too well.

But there wasn't anyone to rehearse with.

So he rehearsed himself, in the bedroom that, now that the war might be over any minute, would probably go back to Max and Benjy.

In a way, the Yiddish speech, though longer, was easier to memorize than the English one. It was just words, that's why—empty sounds that Papa put on sheets of notebook paper, as empty as the words in the blessings and in the reading of the Torah.

The English speech, only half a page long, was another thing.

Jake knew what those words meant.

He wanted to cry when Papa set them down on paper and said, "Use a loud voice, Jacob, when you say these words. Let the whole world hear."

But he didn't cry. It would have been disrespectful and, more than that, detestable for him not to be grateful that Papa had even bothered. That he had found the time, amid all his other troubles, to write the speech at all.

Jake loved him for it, just the way the Fifth Commandment said he should.

The words smarted nevertheless. Jake couldn't put his finger on it exactly, but they smarted. And he trembled at the prospect of having to speak them.

Hannah Rachel's long-kept prayer shawl and silver-covered prayer book were of little comfort.

Jake picked them up at her house the night before the Bar

Mitzvah—satiny smooth tokens of a tradition she finally, now, could perpetuate through at least one more generation of the family—and thanked her for them and promised her he'd cherish them for life and be a man she could be proud of.

The promise made him feel slightly guilty, knowing he'd never go back to a synagogue again—ever.

Still, Jake had to take them to the shop to show to old Izzie. Just to show him. Not to invite him to the Bar Mitzvah itself.

What would have been the point?

Old Izzie didn't believe in empty rituals anyway.

Old Izzie looked at them and then at Jake, murmured something about good luck, and said, "Make it into something, Ackerman. That's all that counts. Don't let it go to waste."

And Jake went back home and rehearsed in the bathroom, watching his lips mouth the two speeches, making them as perfect as he could, without too many *er*s or *uh*s.

When he walked into the Bell Avenue Synagogue that Saturday morning—four days after the invasion of Normandy, at the beginning of what should have been the first day of his life as a full-fledged adult member of that people whom God had chosen—his stomach was knotted up and he had to repeatedly remind himself to keep his voice loud, the way Papa said he should.

He made it through the Yiddish speech without trouble, there being not much of an audience—or Howie—to be frightened of.

But the English speech was another matter. He had to struggle through each word, as though each word were a bigger lie than the one before it:

Dear Friends,

I am very happy at this moment. I thank God that all my brothers are alive on this day of my Bar Mitzvah and that the Allied forces may soon win this war so that soon all my brothers will return home safely and also the sons of all parents will return home safely to an enduring peace all over the world.

That was it. That was the end of it, of the speech Papa had written for *his*—Jake's—Bar Mitzvah.

Some of the few people there clapped as the rabbi pinned the gold, six-pointed Bar Mitzvah medal on Jake's lapel.

Everyone had wine afterwards and egg cookies, and Jake smiled the broadest smile he could.

When it was all over, Jake kissed Mama and Papa, saying, "That was really a great speech you wrote for my Bar Mitzvah, Papa. It made me real proud to be able to say it. Did I do it all right?"

Mama and Papa kissed him—one on either cheek—for an answer.

As the three of them, walking arm in arm back to the apartment, came to Francisco Avenue, Jake, trying hard to hold back the anger and anguish, said, "Is it okay if I stay outside a few minutes?"

Mama, who, now that he was a man, didn't even make an effort to hold his hand anymore, and Papa, who never had, walked on ahead, saying in unison, "Anything, Jacob. Anything you want." Then they laughed proud laughs and added, "You're a man now."

After the two of them disappeared up the front-porch stairs, Jake went to the telephone pole and stood there a minute with his back towards the apartment.

It didn't take but a second to unpin the gold medal from his lapel.

He held it in the palm of his hand with the sun hitting it full on so that it was almost too dazzling to look at.

Chris Petropolous's face was only a blur now. A vague, misty recollection that refused to sit still in his mind.

Jake bent over at the base of the pole, dug a hole, and set the medal into it. He smoothed the dirt over the medal and prayed the only prayer that meant anything to him.

"You're more one of the Chosen People than I am," he prayed.

He got up and walked to the porch, where he found Howie standing.

Howie, seeing the prayer book and blue velvet bag containing the prayer shawl in Jake's hand, said, "Hey, Ackerman. Was today your Bar Mitzvah?"

"Yeah," Jake said.

Howie shrugged. "Geez," he said. "I forgot. You know? I would have come. I just plain forgot."

Jake started climbing the stairs. "It's okay, Howie," he said, "It wasn't any big deal anyway."